TO ~~Christy~~
on Books!

Best always

COVID GALAXY

MARK GOODE

Mark Goode

To purchase books or for more information,
www.lusatropics.com

This book is a fictional work about pandemics. The story is an ancient one repeated throughout history. Unfortunately, we are currently in the throes of the COVID pandemic; however, any resemblance of the characters or stories in this book to real-life persons, places, or events is purely coincidental.

ACKNOWLEDGMENT

—

I want to acknowledge my wife Melinda for graciously creating a kind spot in her heart for me. Also, a special thank you goes out to my editor Christina Palaia of Emerald Editorial Services, for being a seminal influence in my writing. And, finally, thanks to my long-term friend and graphic designer Nikylla Celine for such a beautiful cover and book design.

Thank you all!

DEDICATION

—

This book is dedicated to the healthcare workers battling the COVID pandemic, especially the brave men and women caring for the sick. You are amazing!

Are we alone in the universe?

At a time when Earth is ravaged by a viral pandemic, and world leaders struggle to save humanity from extinction, astronaut and accidental tourist William Preston adventures into the multiverse on an important mission for the Janus — the all-seeing interstellar entities who enact justice across all galaxies. Plucked from his post aboard the space station during a solar storm and thrust unknowingly into other timelines, William fears insanity or the ill effects of radiation until the Janus reveal themselves in a close encounter of the fifth kind.

Is anybody out there? Can you hear me?

Like a message in a bottle, this story, in a tide of electronic bytes, washes ashore on a future Earth in order to awaken the planet's inhabitants to the truth of our galaxy.

Could COVID have come from outer space?

William is set to find out as he pursues the intergalactic criminal Fermion, who is wanted for stealing an eleventh-dimensional galaxy from the Klabyau. In exchange for his help, the Janus promise to locate William's missing wife and love of his life, Maia, who vanished in a freak incident in the New York subway. In the course of his travels, William discovers other beings and other worlds that are also battling a crippling virus.

In a spectacular conclusion orchestrated by the Janus and Klabyau, a new day dawns, the trapped COVID souls are freed, and William and Maia are reunited in a wondrous new existence.

CONTENTS

CONTENTS

—

CHAPTER 1

A Gauntlet Thrown

M om! Dad! Look what I found in the basement!"
Heather Jones Ricci looked up from the box
of dinner plates she was unpacking as young Mark burst
into the kitchen. Like a lot of stepparents looking for
acceptance and trying to assimilate into the culture of a
new family, Heather was thrilled hearing the boy call her
that name. She smiled, watching him charge toward the
kitchen table, clutching a clunky-looking, old-style laptop
computer.

The table was cluttered with crumpled packing paper
and odds and ends she hadn't found a home for yet, so he
elbowed open a spot and set down the computer. They'd
only just arrived here this morning at her family's old lake
house, toting all their household belongings. It would be
their final retreat from the city, the place where they'd wait
out the rest of the pandemic, just the three of them, about

as socially distanced as they could be.

"What have you got there?" she asked Mark, coming up beside him.

"Where's Dad? Dad!" he called. "What is this thing?" The computer was covered with decals of spaceships, galaxies, and nebulae.

Angelo strode into the room, looking curious. His features were relaxed and, despite the chaos of the move, she could see the relief of finally having escaped their beloved once-vibrant city written all over his face. "What's going on?" he asked.

Mark pried open the laptop's lid and was feeling around for the power button. "Do you know anything about this? It was in a box downstairs marked *M-A-I-A*. Whose is it? Can I have it?"

Angelo glanced at Heather, then said, "Let's take a break from unpacking and go out on the deck."

"I wonder what's on this thing," Mark said. "I saw a charging cable downstairs. Think it goes to this? You have to plug into wall electricity to charge devices this old, right?"

Heather laughed. "Yes, back in the Stone Age, we had to actually plug our electronics into an electrical outlet to power them up. Our stuff didn't do ubiquitous charging as yours do."

Mark disappeared down the basement steps again. Angelo picked up the laptop and, with his arm around his wife, ushered her past the moving boxes stacked four high to the ceiling and through the sliding glass doors. "Hurry up!" he called back into the house. "You won't want to miss this sunset!"

"I never realized what a hoarder I had become," Heather said. "All these things we brought with us."

"I know," Angelo agreed. "Where did all this stuff come from?"

Heather settled into one of the Adirondack chairs and propped her feet up. The last half hour of daylight was about to yield to the evening darkness, and a cool breeze kicked up off the water. Across the cove, the Swanson's porch light flicked on. As far as she could tell, they were the only other people staying on the lake. With a frown, she counted the darkened houses along the curve of the shore: the Johnson's, the Young's, the Evans's, the Newton's, the Connor's, the Smith's — all vacant. Yep, that was about right — the unrelenting virus had taken down six or seven of every ten people on the planet. But these were families she had known since childhood, simply wiped out. A shudder ran down her spine. She wondered if she'd ever hear their names again.

Mark dashed out onto the deck, charger in hand. Excitedly, he announced, "Found it! Hey, Mom, who's Maia?"

Heather shot a look at Angelo, then turned back to young Mark. "Maia is an old friend and schoolmate of mine. We worked together at a medical device manufacturer before I started my company," she said. "And that computer belonged to a man named William, our friend, and Maia's husband. He was an astronaut."

"An astronaut?! Cool!" Mark said, running his fingers over the decals on the computer's lid. "But why do you have his computer?"

"Well, uh," she paused. "Unfortunately, Maia and Bill are gone, both having experienced a premature end to their time on this planet. We were very close friends, and Maia's father, Frank, contacted me a while back, before the second wave, wanting to know if I was interested in any of their belongings."

Angelo popped the cork on a bottle of cabernet and tipped some into a pint-size Mason jar for her.

"I agreed to take a look," she continued, "but seeing all their stuff was hard. It conjured up memories of who they once were and the times we'd shared. As a keepsake, I took Maia's violin that she played so beautifully, and Frank gave me one of William's telescopes. Bill loved astronomy and was really into astrophotography. As a matter of fact, he took all those pictures and printed them out as decals," she said, pointing to the lid of the laptop that Mark was marveling at. "Some little voice at the last minute told me I should also take that computer home, and now you've got it."

"Wow, it's old, but can I really have it?" asked Mark. "I

bet there's some cool stuff on here — from an astronaut!"

"I think so," Heather said, looking at Angelo. "What do you think? Perhaps the two of you could try and reactivate it."

"I don't see why not," Angelo replied. "No telling what William left for us to find."

"Cool," said Mark. "It works when I plug it in...."

The computer booted up and displayed the desktop window. Mark navigated around naturally, as if he was already familiar with the outdated operating system, and started exploring what was on the computer. It sported two hard drives, one of which was functioning as the startup drive; the other, however, was encrypted with a password.

"Well, this will be a lot of fun!" exclaimed Mark. "I'm going to play with it and figure out how to hack into the second drive," he said, his fingers busy tapping in code. "Hmm, this computer needs a name. I think I will call it Sirius, like the star." Mark was a kid who willingly spent his free time — of which he had an abundance since remote learning was suspended last year — tinkering with electronics and computers.

Suddenly, they heard a ping from Sirius, and a notification popped up on the screen. Mark quickly opened the email client.

There at the top of the queue, appeared a new message: "If you can break the encryption code, the story, this computer, and its contents are yours!"

"Wow! I wonder who sent that?" exclaimed Angelo. Heather stood behind Mark with her hands on his shoulders, fascinated with how quickly the boy was bringing the old laptop to life.

"I don't know," replied Mark, fingers typing. "The usual identification fields in the metadata are blank."

"That's very strange," Angelo said.

"Look!" Heather pointed to the password box that appeared beneath the icon of the second hard drive. Thinking out loud, Heather reasoned that because William was an astronaut, the password likely had something to do with space, rockets, or possibly his other passion, astronomy.

"Let me take a guess," Mark said, typing in *auroraborealis*. The screen flickered briefly but remained locked. "Hmm, probably have to include upper- and lowercase and symbols and numbers." Then in quick succession, he tried *AuroraBorealis, sup3rn0va, BlackhOle, 5ingularity, multi-verse!*, all unsuccessfully.

A new box labeled *Password Hint* appeared, displaying the words "I Reside Within M16" followed by seventeen blanks.

"Well, it appears as though someone has just challenged you to solve an encryption puzzle," Angelo said. "But I am still curious about the origin of this new message."

"I don't know. I'll need to do some research," Mark said. "I wonder what M16 is?"

"I think that's the name of something you'd find in space, like a star cluster or something," said Heather, "but with a seventeen-character encryption key, the possibilities are immense."

"Agreed," said Angelo. "I wonder if our internet provider could tell us where this message came from."

"There are a lot of astronomy books piled in the same box where this computer was downstairs," said Mark. "I'll see what I can find." He disappeared into the house.

Angelo reached over and topped up Heather's wine. She gave him a tired grin and then spoke into her communicator: "Deck lights on." A bunch of paper lanterns strung across their elevated perch flickered on.

"*The Messier Handbook: Guide to Viewing the Heavens*," Mark announced, striding over to the laptop again. "Maybe this has got a clue in it...." He cracked open an old hardbound book, and Heather caught sight of black-and-white astronomical photos scattered across the pages. The glossy paper in a section of color plates was covered with images of beautiful star clusters and roiling nebulae.

As Mark flipped through the pages, Heather spoke to her communicator: "Trace, tell us about Messier."

The screen light flickered in time with the AI voice: "From *Wikipedia*," Trace intoned, "'Charles Messier was a French astronomer in the eighteenth century. He published an astronomical catalog consisting of 110 nebulae and faint star clusters, which came to be known as the Messier objects.'" Heather cocked her head at Mark, who nodded and allowed the virtual assistant to continue. "From *Encyclopaedia Britannica*: 'In 1760, he began compiling a list of nebulae so that he could distinguish better between nebulae and comets, which look alike when viewed with a small telescope such as was available to Messier. Many of these nebulae, including some of the most prominent, are still known by his catalog numbers, M1 through M110.' From *ConstellationGuide.com*: 'The Messier objects are popular targets among amateur astronomers because they are relatively bright and easy to find on — '"

"Thank you, Trace. Exit," Heather commanded.

"Check this out," Mark said, and then read aloud the handwritten inscription inside the front cover: "'To My Dearest Love on Our Wedding Day, May the stars of the heavens always shine for you. All my love, yours, Maia.'"

Heather reached across and flipped the cover closed so she could examine it. "Oh! This is that rare book! Maia and I found it in an antiquarian's shop just before they got married."

"It looks like he started finding the Messier objects!" Mark exclaimed. "Look!"

Heather and Angelo leaned in closer. Written on the endpapers in an architect's hand was "Messier Marathon" followed by a list, one through sixteen. Heather chuckled, pointing to an accompanying list of hand-drawn stars next to each number. "It looks like they were hunting the heavens together, and Maia was rating their findings." She ran her finger down the list. "Boy, she went wild for M16..."

The last item listed was: "M16: Eagle Nebula in Serpens constellation. Also called 'Star Queen.'" Next to it, Maia had drawn five stars and also scrawled "My fave!!" with a smiley face under the exclamation points.

Mark's eyes flew open wide. "'M16' is her favorite Messier? That's the password hint, too." He tapped the password box and started typing ferociously: *SerpensConstellation*. Nothing happened. "No, that's too long," he said. Then, *M16Serpens, Messier16Serpens, M16EagleNebula*? "No, no, no! Too short." Next, *EagleNebulaCluster*? "Argh! Too many!"

Angelo rested a hand on his shoulder. "Wait a minute, son. The hint is 'I reside *within* M16,' which is her favorite Messier object. What's inside the Eagle Nebula of the Serpens constellation?"

Mark flipped back to the color plates and found the page with various images of Messier Object 16. Prominently displayed in the middle of the page, gigantic spires of lavender, red, and yellow interstellar dust and amorphous gases practically plumed off the page at them. Next to this photo, Maia had drawn an emoji with star eyes. The plate was labeled: *Pillars of Creation*.

Mark quickly counted the characters, excluding spaces, and exclaimed, "Yes! Seventeen." Then he typed the magnificent image's name into the password box, all one-word lowercase. Once again, nothing happened.

He frowned, then brightened and tapped in: *PillarsOfCreation.*

—

CHAPTER 2

William Preston, Astronomer-Astronaut

Sirius's screen blinked, and then a short animation showed cartoon locks and chains falling away from the encrypted drive's icon, which was shaped like a pirate's treasure chest that was creaking open. A message materialized in the middle of the screen:

Hello, my name is William Preston. My friends called me Bill. Like the proverbial message in a bottle floating in the sea — or an orb cast into outer space — I commit these writings to the fate of the universe.

This story is so unbelievable. Telling it would have most certainly brought my career as an astronaut to an end. Not that that is relevant any longer.

I leave this story behind in hopes that it might be discovered someday and provide closure not only for my family but also for humankind. Although hard to comprehend, I have a fundamentally new and different existence now. I am okay. I hope to explain to you here how it all happened, and perhaps I'll attain a different type of immortality as an author.

—

I grew up on a farm in Montana. It would be difficult not to fall in love with the magnificent heavens on display in a state known for its big skies.

Our family spent a lot of time together on frequent camping trips to the mountains. We enjoyed hiking, boating, and fishing. There is nothing quite like a campfire to appease the pyromania in a young boy. With the evening upon us and the nighttime approaching, I looked forward to the ritual of gathering firewood, skillfully arranging kindling in the shape of a pyramid surrounding a wad of newspaper, then watching and waiting for the "Oh yeah!" moment when the fire crackled, signaling success.

Dinner usually consisted of hot dogs and hamburgers, copious amounts of chips, and usually of course, concluded with the ceremonial roasting of marshmallows. The campfire raged on against the enveloping darkness and chill of night. On a clear night, the starlight was sufficiently bright that a flashlight was not necessary. Later on, I would survey the night sky with my father's binoculars from the comfort of my sleeping bag.

For my twelfth birthday, I was given a telescope, which

I often brought along on our camping trips. I was amazed to actually see the rings of Saturn, some of the moons of Jupiter, and the red glow of Mars. The moon, however, never failed to keep me entertained, with its display of mountains, plains, and craters.

In high school, I liked science and was pretty good at math. I took my first real course in astronomy my freshman year of college. Eventually, I would go on to study physics and astronomy; the latter, however, became my passion.

In an attempt to get even closer to the stars, I applied and, by virtue of my good grades and persistence, earned an interview at the Space Academy. I fantasized about becoming an astronaut and dreamt of being a mission commander, piloting a spacecraft into the heavens.

—

Most cadet astronauts, myself included, came from a background of hard science and mathematics. Engineers, physicists, and math nerds are, typically, not the most socially adept group. Likely the only dance steps we knew were those our mothers had taught us prior to homecoming or in preparation for a wedding. While public speaking was not my strong suit, I could do karaoke, but only after more than a few beverages.

I came from Montana, where cowboy boots and tight

jeans could get you into any venue. College life was an eye-opener, for certain, but living in big cities like Los Angeles and New York City, where the astronaut training facilities were, was really an education.

Space Command valued diversity in their cadets. We joked that it would come in handy when talking to a Martian, for instance. We were trained to have an open mind, and we encountered more than a few "aliens" in the city. Of course, we also encountered some interesting creatures in our extensive field training, camping, and hiking in deserts and jungles and on ocean beaches.

For one particular exercise, they dropped us off in the desert near a large crater in northern Arizona. The massive excavation had resulted from the impact of a meteorite eons ago. It amazed me. I was team leader on that exercise, and our goal was to descend the crater to our shelter and supply station at the bottom. It was a technical descent, and we rappelled until the darkness compelled us to bivouac on a ledge. The locals — countless scorpions and rattlesnakes — were not that friendly.

We spent a week down there testing our survival skills and equipment. The night sky was spectacular and reminded me of my younger days camping in Montana. The worst maneuver required us to live in a spacesuit for forty-eight hours, a necessary skill we hoped never to have to utilize.

After that, in my personal time, I turned my attention

to meteor surveillance and hoped to discover and perhaps get my name on one of them.

For a while, I was an astronaut by day and astronomer by night. I made a lot of good friends in the astronomy community and got to visit some great observatories and use their powerful telescopes throughout both hemispheres.

Soon enough, generalist training was over, and I had to complete the latter few months of my specialist training at one of the Space Command's hub facilities, in either LA or New York. During that time, I'd be recruited to a specific mission, and my final preparation would focus on the mission specifics. Then I'd be deployed to outer space.

Although I'd be traveling only a few hundred miles above Earth's surface, space was functionally infinitely far away. To an astronomer, however, it was a dream come true to be given the opportunity to observe the skies from outer space without looking through the Earth's atmosphere. I would have the best vantage point possible.

—

I often wondered whether life existed elsewhere, outside of the magnificent Planet Earth. Of course, at the Space Academy, we considered this question in practically every discipline, from astronomy to zoology. How do we define life? What might we find out there? Would we encounter intelligent beings ostensibly like us, with consciousness and hopefully a conscience, or lesser forms, such as animals, lacking both? How about cells, plants, bacteria, or viruses? What were our chances of "hitting the lotto" and finding someone out there we could talk to?

To my mind, it seemed more likely we would find an alga, fungus, or bacterium rather than a whole developed rational life-form. Perhaps a single-celled organism with the metabolic machinery to process alien nutrients or materials and extract energy that it used to grow and reproduce? But that didn't keep me from hoping.

According to astronomy and cosmology, there are at least a trillion galaxies in the observable universe, each potentially containing a trillion stars or suns. Some of them would *surely* have solar systems and planets similar to Earth. Quantum mechanics and string theory give us even more potential places to look for extraterrestrial life, such as other dimensions and perhaps even a multiverse.

Finding the proverbial needle in a haystack would be easy compared to the task before us. Perhaps "finding an atom in a galaxy" is a better analogy. The scale we were contemplating is literally infinite. The distances are truly immense. With our current technology, if we were to travel through space to our nearest neighboring star, Alpha Centauri, approximately 4.2 light-years away, it would take us about 80,000 years!

Until we can develop the ability to warp space-time or

travel near the speed of light — an everyday occurrence for science fiction writers but considered impossible by physicists — it seems that we are functionally alone.

But are we?

—

CHAPTER 3

Maia, the Love of My Life

In preparation for the astronomy component of the mission of which I was in charge, I flew to various observatories in both hemispheres to collaborate and visit many of the friends I had made in the astronomy community. Then, the last part of my training was scheduled for the Space Academy field office in the smart city of Manhattan.

I had briefly visited New York previously but really looked forward to an immersion this time. The training module would last twelve weeks, giving me a chance to experience the art, music, theater, museums, and cultural diversity of the city.

I arrived on a Friday so I could get situated before starting a full training schedule the following week. The academy sent a shuttle to the airport to retrieve me. Orientation at the Space Academy administrative office in

Midtown lasted a few hours, and basically, all I had to do was clear security, get a picture ID, and take a brief tour of the facility.

I was staying in an apartment within walking distance of Central Park and several of the museums and restaurants I wished to visit. I was excited to explore the metropolis, but the first priority was getting dinner.

Setting out on foot, I walked around, exploring the block my apartment was on. It appeared that the culture of the neighborhood centered around food, fashion, fitness, and pets. Dance studios and gymnasiums were on the higher levels, fit clients dressed for action, easily negotiating the stairways to their sessions looking out over the city. There was no shortage of fashion boutiques and an occasional men's store. The four-legged citizens were well cared for, with abundant pet stores and occasional veterinarian offices. I saw a number of "virtual reality salons" and electronics stores. Bistros and ethnic food from around the globe were well represented. With no shortage of options, I picked an Italian deli based on a rather impressive buffet visible through the front window. As if carbohydrate loading for a marathon, I consumed a sizable portion of rigatoni and meatballs in a luscious deep red sauce, washing it down with plenty of bread and then coffee and a cannoli.

Afterward, I welcomed a long walk around the neighborhood before returning to the apartment and settling in for the night. Looking forward to visiting Central Park the next day, I unpacked my running shoes and then fell right to sleep.

In the morning, I ordered in an espresso and biscotti for breakfast and read the *Times* on my tablet. It was raining, so I deferred running until later that afternoon when the sun appeared. The air was thick and humid, and I ran the paths in the park, dodging people and puddles. After about forty-five minutes, nearing the finish, I sprinted the last hill.

Just as I was leaving the park and about to cross Fifth Avenue, a toddler ran out into the street as the light changed. Simultaneously, an oncoming vehicle rounded the corner. A cacophony of sound rang out, including the panicked scream of the child's mother, tires screeching, and the crowd gasping.

Then, suddenly, a woman on inline skates comes out of nowhere, snatches the child up, jumps the curb, and goes screaming down a dirt trail in the park, amazingly negotiating the rough and exiting onto the adjacent grass, where she sets the kid down.

The crowd cheered when she skated back up the dirt trail and delivered the child to a grateful mother.

"That was totally amazing!" I said.

She turned to see who was talking to her. "Yeah, that was a close call," she said.

I awkwardly stood there looking at her lovely blue-green hair and sparkling eyes. I had only a second to make a connection, so I had to act. I said loudly, "How about a lemonade for Wonder Woman?" to the food truck attendant parked at the curb. "And one for myself."

She grinned and shifted her weight from one skate to the other. On her blades, she was as tall as I was. The crowd picked up on the nickname and started chanting, "Wonder Woman! Wonder Woman!"

"That was quite a performance," I said, handing her the drink. "You saved that kid's life. You're a star!"

She laughed at that.

Then another young woman rolled up, saying, "Hey, Maia, what's going on here?"

"Oh, hi, Heather. Some kid almost killed himself running into the street. This gentleman is buying a round of lemonade."

Heather looked at me. "What's your name, anyway?" she asked.

I signaled the food truck driver for a third lemonade, then, handing the glass to Heather, I said, "I'm William, William Preston. Maia, here, just saved that child."

"Strong work," Heather said, nodding and turning to Maia. Then she chuckled. "Another reason to stick with dogs. At least you can keep them on a leash." Heather turned to me and asked, "What brings you to New York City?"

"I'm here for astronaut training," I replied.

"That's interesting. Maia and I work for a company researching telemetry applications for the space program," Heather said.

"Really?" I was surprised. Of all the people in New York, how about that? "What's the name of the company?"

"Vital Data Management, VDM," Heather replied.

"No way!" I laughed. "I'm supposed to report to VDM on Monday. What a coincidence!"

"I don't believe in coincidences," said Heather.

"Well, perhaps we'll meet again," said Maia. "Thanks for the lemonade!" She turned to her friend and said, "Come on, we had better get moving. We don't want to stand up, Angelo."

I watched the pair skate off. That night, I replayed the scene at the park in my mind, in awe of what had happened. I was fixated upon the whole event and particularly on the woman on skates with the blue-green hair.

—

I ventured out the next day to explore more of the city. I went to the American Museum of Natural History and later found a ticket office where I could purchase one for a Broadway show that evening. I found the VDM offices where I was to report the following morning. I was excited and anxious, hoping I might encounter Maia again.

Monday morning couldn't come soon enough. After a

bagel and coffee, I walked to the VDM office and checked in with the receptionist.

"Welcome, Dr. Preston," she said.

I laughed. "Well, at times, it seems like I have been in training long enough, but I am not a doctor yet," I replied.

"Oh, that's right. You're *only* an astronaut." She laughed. "I see you're here for telemetry analysis and testing. You can sit down here, and someone will be with you shortly."

A few minutes later, Heather poked her head into the reception area and smiled when she saw me. "Oh my," she said, "you're the lemonade guy at the park."

"At your service," I replied. "Small world, isn't it?"

She escorted me to an examination room and then said, "I'll be right back. Maia won't believe this."

Nor could I. It was more than a coincidence, I thought. Returning shortly, she said, "Maia is ready. Follow me."

We entered the exercise lab. Maia got up from her desk and walked over with her hand extended in greeting. "Well, hello, William! What a surprise. I can hardly believe this. It seems like I know you already!"

Heather smiled and patted her friend on the shoulder. "I'll leave you two to it," she said, then exited. It seemed like I'd have Maia all to myself for this session.

"You'll have to tell me more about yourself," Maia said, "but first, I need to collect some health information and vital statistics. Then we'll get you wired up." She wrote down my height, weight, and blood pressure — then proceeded to abrade my skin with sandpaper before placing ECG electrodes.

We would later laugh about that first telemetry meeting when I removed my shirt and modeled my sculpted chest. All those years of working out and going to the gym paid off handsomely.

I was mesmerized by this unique woman. She reminded me of a nebula I had photographed through my telescope, with her striking blue-green eyes and matching hair, which concealed her glittering earrings that invited a second look. The attraction was palpable, eliciting feelings of both enthusiasm and trepidation in me. I was going away in a few months; this was a terrible time to meet someone special.

But I was quite pleased when she informed me that I would need to come back several more times for additional testing. I looked forward to our sessions, scheduled in between my other courses, and Maia occupied my thoughts. She made numerous recordings under various conditions ranging from napping to running. Mondays and Wednesdays, we exercised, and Tuesdays and Thursdays, we analyzed data. We occasionally ran together outside. Maia would wire me with recording equipment before we headed out to the park.

Others in the lab noticed how we seemed to be enjoying one another's company. One day Heather teasingly commented that she was glad we were so invested in the telemetry project.

I had managed to squeeze a Friday afternoon session in, and on this day, we massaged the data using Fourier analysis. Using software, Maia displayed the data as a graph of the frequency spectrum. She said this would help her determine the bandwidth necessary to transmit and process telemetry data.

"You are amazing," I said.

She looked up, and we stared at each other somewhat awkwardly and longer than just a while. Then Maia, smiling, said, "You're fairly amazing yourself."

My heart leaped, and I couldn't keep from grinning. "You know," I said, "our work together will be completed soon. Do you think, perhaps, we might continue to see each other outside of here? I mean, I really enjoy spending time with you."

Her eyes sparkled. "I was hoping you would want to. The answer is yes! Heather and I found this great Italian bistro, and we've become acquainted with the sommelier, Angelo. Would you care to join us this evening?" she asked.

"Absolutely! That would be great!" I responded.

"Okay, good," she said, nodding. "Come by my place at seven, and we can walk to Heather's and take the subway to the restaurant." She spoke her address into my communicator and handed it back to me.

I was super energized as I departed the lab. As I was walking out, Maia had grabbed my hand and reached up to peck me on the cheek. "See you soon!" she said. I must have levitated my way home because I could not remember the walk. Once in my apartment, I checked my email, then showered and got dressed for the evening.

I arrived at Maia's fifteen minutes early and sat outside waiting, watching the seconds tick past on my wrist chrono. The sound of a violin floated from the apartment windows. At 6:59 p.m., I rang the doorbell, and Maia appeared, holding a bow.

"Hi, come on in," she said. "I was rehearsing."

"Wow. You obviously play violin. I did not know that," I said.

"Yeah, since I was about ten years old," Maia said. "I play with an orchestra, although mostly as a substitute. In this town, it's not uncommon for a seat in the orchestra to have two or three layers of backup, and that's me." She settled the instrument into a case lined with blue velvet, then turned to me, gesturing widely. "Sorry! The place is in a bit of disarray." She grabbed a sweater off the sofa and said, "Oh, yeah, we may need an umbrella. They are predicting rain."

Heather lived nearby, only a five-minute walk away. We arrived to find her waiting on the sidewalk, also with an umbrella in hand.

"If it rains, I see I will be in good company," I said.

We walked down the stairs and boarded the subway. After about fifteen minutes, we climbed out and emerged onto a plaza. After another five-minute walk, we arrived at the restaurant. *Ristorante* was scrolled across the front window. A handsome dark-haired man emerged and took both of Heather's hands in greeting. "*Benvenuti!* Welcome! It's great to see you," he said. He looked as excited to see Heather as I was feeling about standing next to Maia. He turned to me, holding out his hands. "And, is this the William whom I have heard so much about? Good to meet you, sir."

I grasped his hand and immediately felt comfortable

with him. Dinner was fabulous, and as the conversation unfolded, I got to know more about Maia and Heather. Angelo visited our table periodically, sitting in an empty chair by Heather and describing the food and wine he had picked out for us to enjoy.

After several hours of fun, Maia said, "It's getting late. I had better think of going home. I have a busy day planned for tomorrow."

"You two go ahead without me," Heather said. "I'm going to stay here and keep Angelo company while he closes up."

We exited onto the street into a light rain. We huddled beneath the shelter of Maia's umbrella in an embrace, not at all deterred by the weather. It was in the back seat of the cab that I kissed Maia for the first time. It was blissful. We awkwardly debated my joining Maia for the night but decided we would meet for a run in the park and breakfast in the morning.

I returned to my apartment, and the wine facilitated a deep sleep.

At 7:30 a.m., the communicator jingled. It was Maia.

"Good morning! — Hope you slept well. That was a great time last night, wasn't it?" Her voice sounded so chipper. "You ready for a run? I was thinking five miles, followed by a visit to my favorite bakery. What do you think?"

We met on the street corner by my apartment at 8

a.m. and then headed over to the park. Maia was in great condition. I had always wanted a companion to work out with, and she was a force to be reckoned with, easily handling an eight-mile-per-hour pace and conversing the entire time. We watched the people, flowers, and birds and breathed the air cleansed by the previous night's rain. Later we sat outside the bakery enjoying breakfast.

"What is on your agenda today?" I asked.

"I'm going to visit my dad and aunt, and I have to practice violin. I'm substituting for a friend in an off-Broadway show tonight," she said.

"Seriously? That's amazing that you're on tonight. Any chance I could hear you play? I would love that," I said.

"Well, I'll be in the orchestra pit under the stage. You wouldn't really be able to see me. But if you really want to, I do have a complimentary ticket if you are interested. Let's go to my place, and I'll get it for you."

My pulse quickened. "That would be awesome," I said.

We climbed three flights of stairs to Maia's small apartment. I looked around and spotted a diploma from a school of nursing. "So, you're a nurse?" I asked.

Maia rummaged through a drawer of the secretary's desk in the living room. "Yes, that is my primary degree," she said. "I started out in engineering, probably influenced by my father, but later switched to nursing. After graduation, I worked in critical care, which is where I became interested in telemetry. Eventually, VDM recruited me, I went into industry, and now here I am!"

An interesting, vibrant painting hung over the kitchen table. A small placard with the title *Kind Spot* accompanied it. I was quite impressed as I read the inscription that described a daughter's love and admiration for her mother. "That is an amazing painting," I said. "Did you paint that?"

"Yes, I painted that as a memorial to my mother." Standing there, a look of sadness swept across her face, and a tear appeared in the corner of her eye. "I'm sorry," she said, shaking her head. "I get emotional this time of year. It's near the anniversary of her death."

My heart ached for her. "May I ask what happened to her?"

"Yeah." A big sigh. "She was killed by a sick, deranged man who was going through a divorce, apparently, and had been using drugs. We still don't know for sure, but it appeared he was attempting to kill his son and estranged wife on the school grounds where my mom was a teacher. Mom shielded the little boy, absorbing the bullets in the process. The coward then shot himself."

"Oh, my goodness! I am so sorry," I said and reached out to enclose her in a hug.

She regained her composure after a minute, then said, "This is the original painting. A print remains on display in the memorial at the school."

"Wow, that is unbelievable. I am so sorry I asked. I didn't mean to bring you down," I said.

"It's okay. My dad says I'm a lot like Mom and that she continues to live on in me. Perhaps you can meet him someday. You and he have a lot in common. He's a forensic propulsion analyst and does predictive failure analysis and testing. He really gets involved when things go wrong."

"Really! That's unbelievable. I look forward to meeting him." It seemed that everything about this woman was just perfect for me.

MY MOTHER IS SPECIAL BECAUSE...
She is kind, understanding, and lovable. She gives me a kind spot in her heart. She shows our family and her friends great care and affection.

Maia retrieved the concert ticket and handed it to me. "Here you are. I'll look for you after the show in the lobby. I am glad you won't be able to see me directly — it might make me nervous!" She laughed. "Well, I had better get moving. I need to clean up and practice for tonight," she said, walking me to the door. Maia kissed me goodbye. "Thanks for the run, and I'll see you tonight."

Once again, I floated home on a cloud of happiness. The show turned out to be a comedy musical set in a tailor's shop, with lots of singing and dancing. The seamstresses and tailors acted out their fantasies through their costume creations, which came to life at night.

After the performance, Maia strolled into the lobby carrying her violin. "Well, that was uplifting," I said. "Oh, and the orchestra was fantastic, particularly the strings section." I handed her a bouquet of fresh hydrangeas. Their color matched her hair almost perfectly.

"Why, thank you!" She plunged her nose into the blossoms and took a deep breath. "Wow, I'm hungry. It's only 10:30. Let's go visit Angelo. Perhaps we can get him to conjure up a late evening snack."

"Sounds good to me," I said. "Lead the way, Wonder Woman."

She looked pleased with her nickname, then disappeared to collect her belongings from backstage.

We hopped the subway and, not surprisingly, found Heather already at the bistro.

"Hi, you two!" she said, jumping up to shuffle a couple more chairs to her table. "How was the show?"

Before Maia could respond, I exclaimed, "It was great! Maia was amazing!"

Her eyes were twinkling, and she entwined her fingers with mine under the table. "Yes, it was a good performance," she said.

From the back of the room, Angelo appeared and spotted us right away. He quickly came over to the table carrying four stem glasses and an opened bottle. We celebrated with a glass of Prosecco, and Angelo came through with seafood penne in garlic pepper and oil. After my unsettled life, moving around the country to finish up space training, I found myself feeling so close to these three good people. I enjoyed their company immensely and was reluctant to think about leaving for my upcoming mission.

After the late dinner, we said goodnight to Heather and Angelo, then walked outside to an awaiting car. We kissed and held hands in the back seat. As we approached her building, Maia said to the driver, "You can let us off here, thank you." She snuggled close and whispered in my ear, "Come on, you're staying with me tonight."

—

After a while, our work at the lab took on a slightly different demeanor. But we were able to conceal our passion from everyone except Heather, who easily saw through the deception.

A few weeks later, we visited Maia's father, Frank, and his sister, Cecilia. It was wonderful to meet them, and they had cooked up a fabulous dinner for the occasion. We had a great time, and Frank and I talked a lot about rocket motors and the future of ion propulsion.

Aunt Cecilia, I would learn, helped raise Maia after her mother's tragic death, a topic that remained difficult for everyone. "I will warn you, William," Cecilia said jokingly.

"Maia takes after her mother: very talented and very stubborn. But her love of music? That comes from me," she proclaimed.

Maia and I were on fire. From then on, we were inseparable. There was no stopping this love train; it had already left the station. We had so much fun! Uncharacteristically, I spent a lot of the money that I had been saving just so we could do activities together. We also went to the park a lot, and Maia taught me to inline skate. I could count at least a dozen Broadway musicals we attended.

I discovered a passion for music, particularly jazz, and we spent hours in the city's many jazz clubs by night and museums by day. There was so much to see and do in this fabulous city. And Maia and I were so in love, we lit up many a venue, our love consuming all the oxygen in the room. Once, a stranger in the park approached and asked if we were married and commented upon the palpable energy between us.

It was then that I realized that I had found the love of a lifetime and that it must be preserved.

The next chance I got, I told Frank how I felt about Maia. We both cried.

"Absolutely," he said, "you have my blessing."

The following Saturday night, my co-conspirators Heather and Angelo and I prepared a surprise. Angelo reserved the most private table in the bistro, and as Maia sat down, I approached her, took her hand, and spoke. "Heather, Angelo, and everyone here as my witness, I have something to say, Maia."

Her eyes widened as she stared up at me.

"Maia," I continued, "from the moment of our first encounter, I have felt a force, unlike anything I have ever experienced. That fateful day, armed with a glass of lemonade, I made contact with a girl sporting blue-green hair and matching eyes who had just miraculously saved a child's life. The universe delivered you, more strikingly beautiful than the most magnificent nebula I have ever seen, to that time and place where I was fortunate to have stood. Maia, I promise to love, honor, and respect you and to hold and protect you. Therefore, I ask if you would consider being my wife and partner." Dropping to my knee, I fetched a ring from my jacket pocket and said, "Maia, will you please marry me?"

She was speechless for a moment. Her cheeks took on a pink blush. She blinked several times and then extended her hand to accept the ring, which I placed on her finger. Then she sprang from her seat and threw her arms around my neck. "What more could a girl ask for than a dreamy spaceman from Montana? Of course I will happily join you on this celestial mission!"

The room erupted with the sound of Champagne corks popping and cheers.

CHAPTER 4

—

Wedding,
Sans Planner

L ife is full of surprises. I never anticipated finding the
woman of my dreams in New York City. My stay
in the city of three months' duration was passing in the
proverbial blink of an eye. I started to resent the idea that I
had to leave to go to the space station in just a few weeks. I
contemplated dropping out of the Space Program, but, of
course, Maia would have none of it.

"You have spent your whole life in preparation for this.
You could not possibly let this opportunity go, and I won't
let you do that," she said.

With that conversation behind us, we focused on the
future and discussed my possibly relocating to New York
City someday. We were having a difficult time deciding when
to have the wedding; something told me sooner was better
than later. Therefore, we scrambled to arrange it before my
deployment. Although the short notice was problematic for

a lot of people we wanted to invite, fortunately, Frank had access to an outdoor venue, and Angelo's restaurant agreed to do the catering.

Heather would be the maid of honor, and my brother agreed to come and be my best man. The rest of the family, unable to travel on short notice, would participate remotely through a series of webcams and screens that Maia and I wired up around the place. We planned to go back to Montana for a celebration the next year after my deployment to the space station.

With the magic day finally upon us, we gathered for the big event. It was a surreal experience.

I could hardly believe it was happening. At one point, it felt like I stepped out of the moment in order to take it all in. Anxiously waiting under the arbor with my brother, Eric, and two astronaut friends from the academy, I took a deep breath. The orchestra was playing Maia's favorite Debussy selection that so beautifully filled the garden.

Silence then descended, and I could feel my heart beating. I took a deep breath as the quiet dissolved in layers of first piano, then harp, followed by more strings, then horns and percussion playing a New Age wedding march.

Maia was stunning, proudly escorted by her father, Frank, both wearing big smiles.

I waited at the end of the garden path. When she arrived, I reached for her hands, and we stood facing each other under the arch. We exchanged our simple, heartfelt vows, and then I slipped a stone of blue sapphire rimmed with diamonds upon Maia's finger.

The whole affair was simple but elegant. Many, including my family, watched the live video feed. After the ceremony, we moved to an adjacent reception area inside a big white tent in case of rain. Eric led off with a toast, which was followed by a few words of congratulations from my parents, courtesy of the video link and large screen over the dais. Angelo's restaurant had prepared a lovely meal for us, but we refused to let him work during the event, holding him hostage at our table.

Maia and I waltzed. Then she danced with her father, and I danced with Maia's Aunt Cecilia. Gradually, others joined us on the dance floor, and the orchestra added guitars and vocals. We danced and danced, burning some calories to make room for wedding cake, an Angelo Ricci creation consisting of luscious, deep red cake with an amaretto cream frosting accompanied by genuine spumoni.

I was in double heaven at that point. We truly had a wonderful day. I would remember it for the rest of our lives. Later and quite exhausted, my new wife and I slipped away to an awaiting limousine and spent the night in a penthouse suite, courtesy of Frank.

CHAPTER 5

—

A Long Countdown
to Outer Space

It was hard to believe that within a few short months, I had found and married the love of my life. With my anticipated departure creeping ever closer, we were uncertain whether we should look for a new apartment together. We decided that, rather than complicate things, we could better spend our time together in the short term alternating between Maia's place and my rental. Living out of two apartments was actually a lot of fun. We continued to go out on dates and enjoy each other and the city.

The good news was that the company Maia worked for, VDM, was awarded the contract to upgrade the biotelemetry for the mission, which meant that I could spend more time "officially" with Maia working on the project. In our work together, we were sure to incorporate a private communications channel that would allow us to visit with one another by video link.

Things were going to get serious with Space Command relatively soon, and the upcoming mission would consume exponentially more of my time and energy. This mission was set up with a significant emphasis on astronomy, hence my presence as mission specialist in the crew. I was slated to set up and manage multiple deep-space astronomical experiments and keep a careful log of observations.

Although life in a space station is not terribly demanding from a physical standpoint, it is important for astronauts to remain physically fit, so Maia and I exercised together frequently. We had a local gym membership and did a fair amount of running and inline skating.

Only about six weeks remained prior to the scheduled launch in Florida. The launch vehicle and spacecraft were already in place on the launch pad, and the engineers and scientists were busily setting up and troubleshooting thousands of details. My presence was required in Florida thirty days prior to launch, meaning I had only about two weeks left with Maia. I was tied up in knots, missing her already.

In the event that one of us should get sick or injured, alternate astronauts were in training at another site in parallel with Russell, James, and I in New York. I won't lie: feigning illness to get out of my twelve-month deployment did cross my mind.

I enjoyed watching Maia, her mannerisms and graceful beauty, present even when she slept.

I confided in her that I struggled with the thought of being away from her. "I have the same feelings and anxiety," she responded. "I have never felt this way either. But at least we can see each other whenever with the video link!" she said.

I would soon have to say goodbye to Maia, my new bride, as the preparation process demanded more of my time.

Space Command shuttled Russ, Jim, and I down to the cape, where we'd spend a good part of the days at the launch site within the command module. I much preferred my daily routine with Maia to spending the days with two sweaty dudes in a tin can, but such is the life of an astronaut. The three of us were given frequent medical examinations and were quarantined for the last two weeks before launch. On two occasions, we did test the telemetry links, and Maia and I managed to also verify our private link. Still, she and I did our evening video chats during quarantine on our communicators since germs couldn't travel through space, or so we thought.

We were in the last ten days of the launch cycle when it happened. A massive solar storm erupted, spewing blasts of high-energy particles that would pummel the Earth within the next few days. Upon arrival, the planet lit up with a massive aurora. This visible show, however, was dwarfed by the unseen bombardment of high-energy particles that disrupted global communications and disabled many satellites. Needless to say, we were unable to launch under such conditions, and the mission was scrubbed.

Space Command did a massive analysis in order to select an alternative launch date. Some planetary alignment requirements needed special consideration. We waited for their decision, and my prayers were answered: the next window for launch was four months out. I rocketed back to New York on the first flight I could get.

Maia was quite happy, and we both felt so fortunate for this unexpected gift of more time together. We quickly fell into our old routines. Maia continued at VDM working with Heather, who confided that she aspired to start her own company someday. The two of them brainstormed about potential products in biomedicine, perhaps a smart defibrillator?

I, for the most part, spent my days at the Space Command facility reviewing star charts and refining my knowledge of star maps and the arrangement of galaxies in the universe. For our wedding, Maia had gifted me a collectible edition of Charles Messier's *The Messier Handbook: Guide to Viewing the Heavens.* I cherished this ancient volume and set a goal to view all of his objects. Unfortunately, the light pollution surrounding NYC precluded deep-space observation; however, through the magic of remote astronomy, Maia and I were able to start our viewing marathon. We took advantage of the high-definition monitors and network available at the facility.

We worked out together daily, mostly in the mornings, but sometimes over the noon hour. When we were not doing astronomy, we went out, occasionally visited Frank and Cecilia, and frequently saw Heather and Angelo. Maia still played with the symphony, and I loved listening to her practice, usually from the adjacent room. We took in a number of concerts, but some of the best times were when we did nothing but talk about and share the more intimate parts of our lives. Eventually, Maia disclosed the details of her mother's murder. It was such a painful and terrible tragedy. I was helpless other than to be there to hold her and listen.

Gradually, we drew closer and closer as a couple. I often got up early and brought her coffee in bed, and then we would sit and talk and plan our day. But then, too soon, we were informed that the launch was definitely scheduled for December 15, when the planetary alignment would be favorable for the astronomy mission. We would have the rest of the autumn, my favorite season, to enjoy together, and I knew the forest colors on the East Coast were rivaled by none, not even Montana's.

On a crisp fall evening, we sat on the balcony with a grand view of downtown Manhattan. We watched birds perform acrobatics diving in and out of the light beams that lanced skyward, presumably snatching moths and other insects attracted to the light.

Maia turned to me with a slight grimace on her face.

"What is it?" I asked.

"Sweetheart, we've just recently experienced the sequelae of the solar storm. Aren't you concerned about exposure to that kind of intense radiation should another storm occur while you're circling the globe in a spacecraft?"

"No, hon, not at all. Our launch vehicle and the space station itself have better-than-adequate shielding to protect us. But I agree, traveling during a solar storm should be avoided — mostly because of the potential disruption in communications, not because of any physiological effects on us biological organisms aboard."

"What do you think a solar flare will look like from space?"

"I think it's going to be pretty spectacular! I can't wait to sight-in more of the Messier objects without the veil of the atmosphere."

"Yes, wow. What do you think the Pillars of Creation will look like from up there?" she asked, pointing skyward. We had worked our way up to M16 in the Messier Marathon, and so far, the dust clouds and interstellar gases within the Serpens constellation were Maia's favorite.

I laughed. "I wish I could take you with me so you can have a front-row view! How I would love to see the stellar winds blowing through your lovely, long matching tresses! We'd sail the heavens together."

"So, I'm married to a sailor and an explorer, aren't I?"

she said. "Only you bring back pictures and data rather than a catch of tuna or other spoils from the sea."

I laughingly agreed and added that I did not plan on running into any dread pirates out there in space. A chill breeze swept over the patio, and we both shivered. "Time to go in?" I asked, standing.

"Speaking of time, it looks as though I have this pirate captive for a few more weeks," she exclaimed as she pounced on my back and planted kisses up and down my neck. "And I intend to cherish every minute!"

"Argh!" I responded in my best pirate. "On that, we are in accord! Let us raise a pint of ale, me beauty, and make a plan!"

"I think I can get a few Fridays off," Maia said. "We could do some long weekends and possibly take in the glorious autumn up north."

"That sounds great," I said. "I wonder if we could fit in a trip to Montana?" I flopped onto our bed and rolled around to face her. She was still giving out kisses, and I returned them in kind.

—

The next thing I knew, we were on a plane to Montana. My brother Eric picked us up at the airport, and I knew something was up when we drove into the ranch, and I saw cars parked along both sides of the long driveway.

Everyone cheered "Surprise!" when we walked into the house. Mom immediately pried Maia off my arm and took her around to meet everyone. Maia was so lovely, and I was so happy that she could finally meet my side of the family. On Saturday, we showed Maia around town. I spotted the old museum and recalled how we'd go there when I was a kid. "Is that grizzly bear still on display?" I asked my dad.

"I imagine so," he said. "Let's go see. Maia won't believe how big that durn thing is."

Once inside the rustic old building on Main Street, we saw the magnificent creature was still standing in the same place, towering over the room.

"Wow!" Maia said, taking a step back. "That is scary! I would not want to meet that monster in the wild."

That night we lit a bonfire out back and grilled steaks and salmon. Dad brought out my old childhood telescope, and I showed Maia the rings of Saturn.

"So, this is where it all started?" asked Maia.

"That's right," I said, showing her how to adjust the focus. "We can also see Jupiter and a couple of its moons, although with this, my first small but mighty telescope, not much detail." As she stooped to look into the eyepiece, I watched her eyes literally light up with "starshine." My chest tightened at the thought of spending twelve months away from my best friend and lover. Although only a few hundred miles away, with no way to return, it was functionally infinitely far. She made everything new for me, and her boldness and zest for life echoed through my soul. Even though my deployment would be packed with new views of the galaxies and stars, I found myself looking forward to its end and my return Earth-side, where I could get on with my happily married life.

On Sunday, Maia and I, needing some exercise after all the extravagant food, went for a run out on the rangeland. Then we met everyone in town for brunch, and I saw more old friends in the lobby of the majestic Big Sky Lodge.

Later that afternoon, we had to say goodbye to everyone. There were lots of hugs, and I kissed Mom goodbye. Maia warmly thanked Mom, Dad, Eric, and the rest of the family for such a warm reception, and they made her promise to bring me back home at the completion of my space mission. As we departed, she waved out the window and called, "We can't wait to come back!"

Soon, we were on the plane. Although we'd be traveling at supersonic speeds, we would still arrive home late. Maia placed her pillow on my shoulder, snuggled up, and fell asleep. A deep contentment crept over me, and I watched the twilit sky envelop us as we hurtled east, leaving the sunset behind.

—

With my departure date rapidly approaching, Maia said, "I have a great idea: let's invite Angelo and Heather over for dinner. It'll be fun to see them outside the restaurant, so Angelo won't be working. I can make my porcini lasagna. It's fabulous!"

I was onboard. We chose a weekday so Angelo could get away from the bistro, and the four of us shared the evening feasting upon Maia's lasagna, then Heather's homemade tiramisu, and of course the wine selections choreographed by our private sommelier, Angelo. The night ended with a toast to my upcoming mission and safe return, and thus, the last week before my departure ended all too soon. Maia took me to the airport, and, like the newlyweds that we were, we sat in the car and kissed and embraced for a long time before I tearfully gathered my gear and left.

Ahead of me in Florida waited my fellow astronauts and two weeks of quarantine. During our seclusion, we spent the days going through every last detail of the spacecraft and our mission objectives. The best part was that I started and ended each day visiting with Maia via a video link.

Russ, Jim, and I triple-checked thousands of items and ran through countless emergency procedures. We also logged an untold number of simulations for the launch and docking maneuvers. The last few days before launch, we spent inside the spacecraft.

Finally, on launch day, in the predawn glow, with the fueling of the rocket completed, we entered the command vehicle and settled in. Three separate computing systems running in parallel processed all data passing in and out of the spacecraft via satellite link. We needed the all-clear from every linked system and monitoring organization before we would get a green light for launch.

I was strapped in with a five-way smart harness that also transmitted my vitals and sent relaxing electric pulses through my muscles. Russ and Jim were similarly secured, with their backs to the ground, staring at the display panels arrayed before them. I heard the countdown faintly inside my helmet: "T-minus ten. T-minus nine. T-minus eight. .." I realized a lifetime of preparation had gone into this moment. "T-minus three. T-minus two..." Maia's face floated before my inner eye. I sent a silent prayer out to the universe for our safe reunion twelve months hence.

"T-minus one. Ignition!"

The engines blasted to life, and the controlled explosion underneath us roared in our headsets. My body being pressed forcibly into the seatback confirmed Einstein's principle stating the equivalence of acceleration and gravity. Within three minutes, I envisioned that we had crossed our own event horizon, indistinguishable from falling into a black hole, except we hoped to emerge alive!

At last, the twilight of space darkened the windows of the command module, and the G-forces eased. The thruster module detached with a metallic clunk, and we were sailing smoothly through the vastness of space. Russ,

the pilot and commander on this deployment, was the first
to unlatch his safety harness and wave me over to unscrew
his helmet.

"Let's settle in here," he said. "It's going to be a long
flight to the station."

It took two days to chase down the space station, and
with the necessary course corrections and flight maneuvers,
we docked successfully on our third day in space. Although
we had confidence in our spacecraft and training — having
bet our lives upon them — collectively, we took a deep sigh
of relief once safely aboard our new home.

—

When I was a kid pretending I was an astronaut living
on the space station, surprisingly, my rendition of station
life, camping out in tents connected by tunnels, was quite
accurate. Our new quarters were not spacious, but we had
everything we needed, and it was within arm's reach. As
ranking members of our crew, Russ and Jim were assigned
individual sleep pods. I, on the other hand, being a mission
specialist, simply tethered my smart sleep sack to a wall
near a window in an out-of-the-way module and set up
camp inside. Weightless inside the sack, and with as much
privacy as could be mustered in a crowded vessel, I could
power up my laptop and catch up on documenting the
day's astronomical observations or write messages to beam

back to Earth or prepare for a video call with Maia.

Our companions, nine other astronauts from Russia, China, and India, had graciously welcomed us onboard with the traditional nonalcoholic Champagne. They squirted small globules of the drink in front of us, and we had to slurp them in before they floated away. It felt a bit like bobbing for apples back on the farm.

Our first "night" there, Jim experienced a tiny bout of space sickness; Maia's telemetry link alerted his assigned healthcare custodian at Ground Control with the first aberration in his vital stats, and he was given specific instructions on how to dose himself with promethazine. He promptly fell asleep in his pod while I climbed into my sack and calculated the time when I could contact Maia through our video link. The station would be passing within line of sight of Manhattan just an hour before we were scheduled for breakfast; my call might rouse her from bed, but I surmised she wouldn't mind since we hadn't spoken since I'd been in space.

"Hi, honey," she beamed with a smile. "It's great to see your face. I love you!" she said.

"I love you, too, and I miss you already," I replied. "The launch was perfect, and we are now safely in our new home. Tell me about your day," I asked.

"Well, I had a nice visit with Dad for lunch. Of course, he says hello. He is so proud of you! He brags about you to his friends quite often. Things are going smoothly at work. Nothing is new to report there. Heather and I are contemplating a visit to see Angelo at the bistro and perhaps a visit to a new art exhibition that is all the rage."

"That sounds like great fun. I'm sure you three will have a blast! You know, I think Heather and Angelo would make a good pair," I said.

"I agree," Maia replied with a huge smile. "I have a suspicion they have a secret relationship we don't know about…"

"Well, it's about time!" I was happy for my friends. Heather and Angelo had become like family to me, and the thought of them as an official couple warmed my heart. They deserved all the happiness in the world. "On that note," I said, "let's visit some more tomorrow. I'm starving and need to get some nutrition, perhaps liquid lasagna." I made a face. "Good night, my dear. I love you."

Maia signed off, making her fingers into the shape of a heart, and blew a kiss.

Lacking the familiar cues provided by the morning sunrise and the evening sunset on Earth, the days seemed to imperceptibly morph into one another. We adapted to the host crew's daily routine quickly, rising at 6 a.m., according to Universal Time, eating breakfast together, getting on with our individual experiments and crew objectives, and then breaking for lunch and dinner together. My eyes were continually dazzled by the multiple sunsets and sunrises the space station "fell" through, and to catch Earth rise out one of the windows was particularly spectacular. We regulated the amount of light passing through the windows of the space station, blocking them completely at the same time each day to simulate nighttime for better sleep; it also provided a welcome break from the never-ending light show of space.

I looked forward to a daily video chat with Maia. She frequently commented that the passing days seemed much longer in my absence and that she missed me. The feeling was mutual, even if my days were filled with magnificent views of the universe around us and of stars being born. She asked if I had clocked any more Messier objects and what they looked like from this totally novel perspective, and I had to tell her no, my count was stuck on M16, the last glorious object we had viewed together. "I'm sure some phenomenal sights still await you, my love!" she said.

Thanks to the video feed, at least I could catch sight of Maia's face nearly every day, phenomenally beautiful to me, and it always made me smile.

CHAPTER 6

A Miracle in the Subway

As the week progressed, Maia and Heather looked forward to their upcoming dinner and visit with Angelo.

"*Buena sera*, Heather. *Buena sera*, Maia," said Angelo as they walked into the restaurant. "As always, welcome. It's great to see you. Good news! I have an excellent Chianti that my uncle found; he was able to buy 120 cases. I really like it. It is sort of bubbly and very drinkable! Let me pour you a taste?"

"Absolutely," said Heather.

"And you, Maia?"

"Well, I think I would like to start with a Prosecco before moving into the red zone. But I am in the mood for your house-special meatballs, you know the ones in that luscious red sauce, over penne, perfect with Chianti, I would think."

Heather and Maia were there almost three hours when they realized the Chianti was speaking to them. "Good thing we're not driving," they said simultaneously.

"Don't worry," Angelo said. "I will get you a ride."

"Well, then, I'll need a limoncello," Maia said.

Another hour later, Angelo escorted them to the curb. He subtly kissed Heather on the cheek before she got into the car.

"It was great seeing you both. I am missing William, though. Come back soon," he said.

The two rode off into the night. Maia pulled out her communicator and pretended to query the virtual assistant. "What does it mean when the waiter kisses you on the cheek?" Then, answering herself, she announced in another voice, "Oh my goodness! It's very clear, my dear, Angelo has the *hots* for Heather," she said, bursting out laughing.

"Well," said Heather, "he is no doubt an outgoing, loving Italian man. We'll see. It was probably the wine, but should he try again, I'm not stopping him!"

The next day Maia reported back to William during their video chat. "The evening was a lot of fun," she said. "There's definitely a romance brewing between Heather and Angelo."

"They'd be a great couple," William agreed.

"Oh, and by the way, we confirmed the art exhibition," Maia said. "It features a large collection of Impressionist art, my favorite. I'll be sure to take a picture of *Starry Night* for you."

William smiled. "Well, I have seen a lot of stars recently, but I would welcome a different perspective. I wish I were there with you," he said. "Have fun, good night, I love you."

And they signed off.

—

At work, Heather and Maia's conversations buzzed with talk of the upcoming Impressionists' exhibition. They were both excited to go — but probably for different reasons. Angelo met them at the entrance to the subway station near Heather's apartment. As the trio descended the steps, they spotted a man lying on the floor near the turnstiles at the entry to the train platform. A few bystanders looked on as he appeared to be having a seizure. One person was speaking into a communicator, summoning an attendant.

Maia gasped when she recognized her father lying prone on the cement. "Dad!" she screamed, then launched into crisis mode and rushed toward him. Heather grasped Angelo's arm with both hands. "Please, Angelo, run for help!" and she dashed off to follow Maia.

Falling back upon her critical care background, Maia tried to get a response from her father. "Daddy, Daddy, are you okay?" she asked, shaking and trying to arouse him. "Talk to me," she said, but there was no response. His jaw was clenched, and his face was blue. She checked his pulse but felt nothing. Heather leaped toward the AED station and returned with the device, which she handed to Maia, who quickly connected the electrodes to her father.

Maia delivered several countershocks with the defibrillator, and they took turns compressing his chest and delivering breaths of air. Maia coached her father: "Come on, Dad, you can do it," she said. In her desperation, she probably delivered more shocks than recommended, but who was counting.

"I hope the paramedic arrives soon," Maia said to Heather. But neither Angelo nor an emergency services technician was anywhere to be seen.

Finally, at the point of exhaustion, with tears and sweat raining down upon her father, Maia cried out, *"Please, dear God, please do not take my father! Take me instead! I will do anything! Help us!"*

Strangely, the lights flickered as Maia delivered one final shock, then darkness filled the entire subway. Heather froze.

It seemed like an eternity, but she saw beams of light sweeping across the scene, and then Angelo arrived, leading the paramedics with their powerful flashlights. Just as they approached, the space roared back to life: the power came back on, and the buzz of the crowd returned.

A cloud of smoke rising from the spent defibrillator lingered over the scene, but Maia was missing. Heather stood up and turned around and then whirled back to look the other way. "Maia? Maia?!" she shouted.

Angelo moved to her side.

"Where did Maia go?" she asked repeatedly.

"I don't know," Angelo replied. "Maybe she had to go to the bathroom?"

"Not a chance!" Heather exclaimed. "She would never leave her father!" Heather started sobbing. "Something is wrong. I feel very hot," she said, then collapsed to the ground.

Angelo had just enough time to catch her before her head hit the floor. One of the paramedics rushed over to see what had happened. The others continued working on Frank, who was now moving and showing signs of life. Within a matter of minutes, the paramedics loaded Frank and Heather onto gurneys and rushed them up and out of the subway, leaving Angelo bewildered and alone to talk to the police and look for Maia.

An immediate search of the area failed to locate Maia. The working theory was that Maia was abducted in the darkness of the power outage. Surveillance video confirmed the beginning and end of the event, showing Maia working on her father when the lights went out and then her absence afterward, as described by Angelo and others at the scene. The cameras had captured a good likeness of Maia.

After he answered as many of the investigators'

questions as he could, Angelo left the subway to attend to Heather. At the hospital, the evening news was already reporting the mysterious disappearance of "a Good Samaritan" who had stopped to assist a man in need and disappeared in a cloud of smoke during a momentary power outage. The news showed a photo of Maia that had been copied from the VDM website in hopes that someone had seen something.

Heather woke up in a hospital bed to find Angelo sitting beside her holding her hand. His worried eyes widened when she looked at him and smiled weakly.

"Oh, Madonna!" he exclaimed softly. "Thank God you're back." He squeezed her hand.

Her head rolled back to center, and she stretched. "What happened? Where's Maia? Where are we? What happened to Frank?"

"Whoa, whoa, slow down," he said gently. "You're at Mount Sinai. You fainted. They think it was a stress reaction. Frank had a heart attack, but he survived, and the doctors have placed a coronary stent."

She sat up straighter in the bed. "And Maia? Where's Maia? Is she okay?"

Angelo looked down at their entwined fingers. "I'm so sorry, Heather. We cannot find Maia. The police searched the gallery, the restrooms, even the maintenance tunnels under the tracks, but they did not find a trace of Maia. It's as if she just vanished!"

—

We understood that additional power outages and disruptions plagued the planet that night as the result of another large solar storm. On the space station, I had my hands full dealing with the situation. In the back of my mind, Maia's concerns about my safety outside the Earth's protective atmosphere played out.

In place of our daily video chat, on the day of the storm, I received a communication from Maia. I was too busy to break for sleep that night but was taking my shift helping the rest of the crew monitor the solar shields and all the external technology while we were bombarded by photons and energetic particles hurled at us by the solar storm. I had just enough time to glance at her message. She had sent a picture of *Starry Night* from the art exhibition along with a text stating, "Hi, honey, I just wanted to let you know that I love you and that I am okay."

I was surprised her message was able to get through at all. In a down moment later in the night, I tried to call her but was unable to establish a link, not unusual given the circumstances of a solar flare.

Multiple detectors outside the space station were registering high levels of radiation, but inside, protected by the shielding, levels were close to normal. Curiously, one of my experiments looking for exoplanets registered some peculiar readings, as if the entire space station had passed into the "shadow" of something.

I glided to an observation window. Astonishingly, I came face-to-face with what appeared to be an enormous spacecraft illuminated by a shower of radioactive particles. I reached for my recorder to get a photograph, but the apparition quickly vanished.

I grabbed ahold of a tether near the window to steady myself. *Holy moly!* Had I just made first contact? I shook my head and peered out the window again. Empty space, lit only by the glow of an upcoming dawn, was approaching as we rounded on Earth. Probably not, I reasoned, concluding that I had most likely seen some anomaly of the solar storm.

I turned and observed the other crew members scattered about the main module. They all appeared immersed in their tasks, unperturbed. They obviously hadn't seen anything out of the ordinary. Then I swiveled back to the window and confirmed: there was nothing there.

A few hours later, the shower of radiation pelting the space station waned, and we were able to re-establish our communication links with Ground Control. I thought I'd take the opportunity to also try to reach Maia so I could hear how her outing with Heather and Angelo had gone. I tried a number of times every few minutes but was unable to connect. That wasn't like her. She carried her communicator with her at all times just on the chance that she and I would have the opportunity to connect. A stone dropped in my stomach. I decided to ask Mission Control to troubleshoot the telemetry link, suggesting that Heather be contacted.

—

Heather was discharged from the hospital the next morning. But she was distraught, unable to focus on anything but a plan to search for Maia. "What about William?" she asked. "Has anyone let him know? He has a right to know!"

Angelo didn't know what to say. "Do you think they would share such news with a husband about a wife when the husband is so far away?"

"I need to talk to him," she said. "I'll tell him. He needs to know."

She contacted the Space Command field office in Midtown and made her concerns known. The officer she spoke with was quite worried about his young astronaut upon hearing the news. A family crisis of an active-duty astronaut stationed in space for an extended period had not happened previously. It was impossible for William to return. The truth was that Maia had disappeared, and they had no explanation of the events that had transpired and so could do nothing but inform and support.

Heather volunteered to be the liaison to her friend, and after much discussion and a background check, it was decided that by virtue of their relationship to their astronaut and his wife, Heather and Angelo would be included in communications with William concerning this topic.

—

"Communications are back up," I announced to Russ and Jim. "In fact, incoming! Ground Control is requesting a video chat now."

The two astronauts floated over and hovered behind me as I established the link with the Earthbound command center.

The communication opened with the presidential seal. I swiveled around and gave a funny look to my compatriots, who both shrugged. Why would a routine message start off so formally?

Then President John Workman himself appeared on-screen and addressed us, thanking us for our service to the country. His manner was so somber that I feared something bad had happened, such as a nuclear war.

Then the general and commander of Space Command, who was sitting beside the president, spoke: "William, I need to inform you about a situation down here on Earth." My insides turned to jelly. Why was I being called out specifically?

"There is no good way to convey this other than directly and truthfully. Your wife, Maia, is missing. She disappeared in a bizarre incident yesterday in the subway during the solar storm. We presume she has been abducted. She vanished without a trace. We have not been able to find her. Your friends Heather and Angelo were there and witnessed the events surrounding Maia's disappearance, and they are here now, as well, to explain what happened."

I involuntarily pushed back from the laptop and crashed into Russell, who put his hands on my shoulders to steady me. It was too much to take in. Incomprehensible. Disappeared? Vanished? None of it made sense.

President Workman then spoke: "William, I know this must be shocking, and I am sorry. The process of working through this news will be difficult, but before we turn this over to your friends, I want to assure you that we are actively investigating, and we will get to the bottom of this. In the meantime, know that we are here for you, and I personally thank you again for your service to our nation."

I stared at the screen. My mind felt numb. Then Heather and Angelo appeared. They tried to maintain their composure as they replayed and related the events in the subway. By the end of it, Heather had her face in her hands and was sobbing in frustration, and Angelo had his arm around her.

I was shaken to the core. "That's so unbelievable. It's crazy. We have to find her," I said, fighting back tears and trying to remain focused. "So, tell me, you never made it to the art exhibit?" Angelo shook his head. "But I got a message from Maia, a photo of *Starry Night*, and she said she was okay. But you never made it there?" I quickly screen-shared the image of the famous painting and Maia's brief message.

Heather and Angelo were speechless. Then Heather said, "No, no, we never made it to the Met."

"We must remain vigilant," I said. "We *will* find her. We have to!"

The commander appointed a liaison for me to speak to daily regarding the investigation and ordered daily counseling sessions, but I refused them. Finally, he granted Heather and Angelo clearance to freely visit with me via the video link.

—

To some extent, my demanding schedule provided a respite from the pain. At night, alone in my sleep sack, I had to go deep inside to find a survival strategy. I requested the full report of the investigation, including the timeline of the events that day and video footage.

Grieving and deeply saddened by my apparent loss, I went about my duties woodenly, Maia never far from my mind. I just could not let it go — not being able to resolve her disappearance with any logical, rational explanation made it surreal. I confided in Heather that I took solace in the fact that Maia's last communication said she was okay; that gave me a reason for hope. However, I could not reconcile the timeline, which revealed that Maia had messaged me and sent the *Starry Night* photo *after* her recorded disappearance on Earth, both impossible.

In reality, I was heartbroken. I cried in the privacy of my sleeping space and during conversations with Heather. I felt helpless, was frustrated, and wanted to return home to look for Maia ASAP.

CHAPTER 7

—

Back Home

J ohn Workman was first and foremost a businessman.
From humble beginnings, he made his start working
for his uncle's accounting firm while he was in high
school and college. He earned a bachelor's degree in
business and entered the job market. He worked for a
telecommunications firm, helping out in the corporate tax
department. It took him a few years, but he completed his
MBA and shortly thereafter earned certifications as a CPA,
a task that took most others several years to complete.

Workman enjoyed the field of corporate taxation.
It involved regularly meeting with some of his former
classmates who worked for the Internal Revenue Service
and wound up on the other side of the table. Sometimes
he would educate his opponents on a particular facet of
the tax code, and other times they schooled him; but in
the end, they would negotiate a settlement and payment

structure as both sides attempted to understand and implement the tax law.

Over the years, he worked for several different global corporations. Building upon his successes, he ascended the corporate ladder to become CEO of a large mining and energy conglomerate. When he assumed the helm, not only the country but also the world was at a crossroads, demanding a new approach going forward to deal with global warming, climate change, and the increasing need for energy by the growing populations. Workman was able to demonstrate that, through innovation, research, and development, he could move the needle toward sustainable energy policy and simultaneously create opportunities for the sidelined coal miners, oilfield workers, mechanics, and laborers and get them back to work. His success earned him a cabinet position in the Department of Energy. And that's how he got into politics.

Politically, he leaned conservative, so the conservatives thought that they could capitalize on his success and popularity in support of the upcoming campaign for the presidency. Workman accepted the nomination for president and asked his steadfast ally Robert Cole to join the ticket. Together, they had mounted a solid campaign, and, as predicted by the conservative party, the voters rewarded them with a victory at the polls.

Early in the term, they already had a number of important political achievements under their belt. The economy was booming, and unemployment rates were at a new low. This was music to the ears of the former businessman and tax executive John Workman. When the first reports of the virus appeared in other countries but were largely discounted by the authorities, Workman was reluctant to interfere with the humming economy and rising standard of living his citizens were enjoying. But astute and ambitious physicians and infectious disease experts could not be silenced; they sounded the alarm and continued to report the case numbers for the new undiagnosed and potentially fatal illness, despite facing sanctions from their own governments.

As measured in travel time, the world had shrunk. A trip around the world could be completed in less than twenty-four hours. With an asymptomatic incubation period of about one week, the virus had a head start. In countries where the first cases were discovered, quarantine and isolation procedures had been implemented. Regardless, within one or two months, cases appeared in every country around the globe.

The infectious diseases and epidemiology experts recommended aggressive action, including a shutdown of the country in hopes of isolating the virus into extinction. Vice President Cole was designated as the point person who would evaluate reports and recommendations from the White House's advisors. He and John had many deep discussions, and they jointly decided that the economic impact of shutting down society was too high a price to pay to slow the spread of a natural virus. Instead, they placed their faith in the hands of modern-day medicine to deal with the new "influenza."

The consequences of this decision became evident over the next several months. The virus devastated the country and almost every other country around the world. Wave after wave of ever-increasing infection rates and deaths occurred. The country was brought to its knees, forcing the governmental authorities to recognize the severity of the illness. The public was demanding some sort of coherent action plan.

Hospitals soon were overwhelmed with cases. There were two and three patients in every room. The staff worked valiantly to the point of exhaustion. Ultimately, makeshift hospitals sprang up everywhere. With resources and personnel pushed beyond the breaking point, an exhausted world strained to care for the sick. Yet death rates skyrocketed, and loved ones were forced to leave their spouses or parents to die alone in intensive care units.

—

Space Command moved up our return schedule, allowing me to return three months sooner than originally planned, during a period of favorable orbital overlap. I was admittedly having problems focusing on work, the search for Maia consuming my thoughts, and so began counting the days. As our departure date approached, I wrapped up my experiments as best I could and left things in order for the next crew.

Russ, Jim, and I undocked from the station in the command module and adjusted our orbit in preparation for the return home. The reentry burn was uneventful, and the spacecraft streaked through the atmosphere to a smooth landing. Once on Earth again, we were examined by the medical team and placed into the mandatory two-week quarantine. My muscles were weak despite my regular exercise on the space station, so I did lots of push-ups and pull-ups to regain strength under gravity. A torrent of administrative work downloading data and documenting the mission thankfully ate away the hours of our enclosure, but I shouldn't have been so anxious to be released into this very uncertain new world.

The world I returned to was much different from the one I had blasted off from the previous year. Not only was Maia gone, but also reports were flooding in of a new contagious illness that was rapidly spreading around the globe. Newspapers quoted President Workman as saying the government and national health centers were "actively investigating." It seemed to me he might say that about a lot of things; whether this investigation turned up results remained to be seen.

My father-in-law, Frank, picked me up from the field

facility. He clasped me tight, and we cried together, both in joy and sorrow. Otherwise, he appeared well and stated that he had made a good recovery from his heart attack. We drove to his house for dinner with Cecilia. The home-cooked meal was unbelievable; every bite brought an explosion of tastes and smells I had been deprived of for so many months in space. We gave thanks and tried to cope with the difficult moments of tearfulness.

That night, not really ready to return to an empty apartment, I stayed at Frank's house. The next morning, a rich cappuccino and homemade biscotti greeted me. I could hardly think of a better way to get the day off to a good start.

My next stop would be home for the task of sifting through Maia's personal effects. No new leads had appeared, and the investigation was dead in the water. I had to face facts: she wasn't coming back, and I had to try to reconcile with her loss. Thankfully, Heather and Angelo met me there. We thought we would first take an inventory of the house before we started sorting. In a room where Maia had kept the memorabilia of her short life, we found her violin, but we were speechless when we confronted *Kind Spot* hanging over the kitchen table. Heather and I wept and decided we were not ready for this examination of Maia's life.

"You know," I said, wiping my sleeve across my eyes, "I think this should wait for another time. I think it might be best if I return to Frank's." We agreed to retreat and re-meet for dinner at the bistro that night, a suitable tribute to Maia.

I returned to Frank's house and sat and surveyed the news. The latest headlines included updates on the mysterious illness. Apparently, doctors had become suspicious of what appeared to be a viral pneumonia that defied diagnosis. Conventional testing had exonerated all the usual suspects. This virulent and contagious respiratory illness was speculated to have arisen in penguins or seagulls and had been carried around a planet shrunken by international air travel, resulting in rapid dissemination around the globe.

The list of experts pontificating on the situation was long and mighty, including specialists in the fields of microbiology, virology, epidemiology, and infectious disease.

President Workman had requested meetings with the major public health institutes and regulatory agencies so that he might learn more about the topic. Historically, the world had experienced pandemics before, some dating back thousands of years. The "*Bible*" described multiple "plagues." These grim accountings chronicled the repeated, futile attempts of society to cope with epidemics that exacted a high toll.

The historical record would reveal that denial was a common response. Governments sometimes denied the existence of a plague even in the face of incontrovertible facts. Also established was the greater toll plagues took on the essential workers necessary to keep society open and on those of lower socioeconomic status, who lived in conditions of poverty and overcrowding.

Tonics, perfumes, coverings, and poultices made of all manner of ingredients imbued with special powers had been utilized throughout history, and it was no different with this current pandemic. Some were inhaled, other concoctions were drunk, and some were applied topically.

Evacuations and retreat were also common responses, but often the contagion accompanied those who were susceptible wherever they went. The evidence preserved in records of long ago vastly exceeded the world's short-term memory and myopic vision. In reality, the grandparents and great-grandparents of those living today had endured and survived the carnage inflicted by many infectious diseases, including smallpox, polio, malaria, measles, and HIV/AIDS, to name but a few. Astute physicians and public health officials who remembered lessons learned from those plagues moved quickly into action, reporting and recommending containment measures to President Workman and Vice President Cole.

I couldn't believe I had returned to a planet in such a wrecked state. Each day more bad news surfaced, and I almost began to believe it was best that Maia was no longer here because I would have hated to see her radiant good health and zest for life constrained in any way.

—

Now that Space Command had given me a leave of absence for mental health, I followed the news as closely as possible. It became a morbid hobby to map and trace the devastation wrought by the advancing virus. Densely populated areas quickly became epicenters of this new plague. Healthcare facilities were strained to the breaking point, and images of bodies piling up graced nearly every broadcast.

The experts quickly identified the infectious agent, and the medical world went into a frenzy looking for treatments. Desperate times called for desperate measures. A number of controversial drugs and treatments were tried — their use was advocated based on limited evidence and anecdotal reports. To my mind, it seems like whenever hard evidence is lacking, public opinion, hearsay, and, ultimately, politicians will quickly fill the void, as if they could legislate a pandemic out of existence.

No known effective medical treatments or vaccines were available. "Use common sense" was the mantra, with efforts aimed at defining the mechanism of spread and trying to "head it off at the pass." Quarantining, social distancing, masks, gloves, and antiseptics appeared to be the only defense. Pandemics are the great social equalizer, a true reminder of the fragility of the human condition. Anyone who breathed air was susceptible. Social status and wealth could help one weather the storm but conveyed no protection from the infection. No one was really immune to the disease.

Thus, the stage was set. The epidemiologists painted the picture of the pandemic with large brushstrokes of red ink and exponential curves of infection rates and mortality. Society, as we knew it, would have to shut down in order to slow the spread.

The world was such a disaster. I soon contemplated a return to outer space, where I could hide from all of this drama, pain, and suffering. I had a lot of work to do to reconcile the loss of my wife and cope with my new way of life in addition to facing the potential end of normal society.

One afternoon, I turned up at the Space Command field office and enjoined the help of the lab technicians there. Using analytical techniques, we studied the video footage from the events in the subway. It was as if I was watching an orchestrated magic show with my wife, Maia, performing a disappearing act. The lights and the smoke seemed to be part of the performance; however, Maia never returned for the accolades from the audience. Further analysis of the eerie images failed to provide answers. One theory the lab techs put forth was that Maia had boarded or was abducted onto the departing train that had arrived just as the lights went out. Abducted by whom? I thought. But, admittedly, that seemed the most likely, and eventually, it was the theory embraced by the authorities.

That night, I had dinner with Heather and Angelo. As usual, we remembered Maia with a ceremonial glass of wine. Happily, their relationship had grown closer and helped sustain them as they struggled to keep afloat with all that was going on.

The next day, in need of a diversion, I turned to the skies. I had purchased telescope time on the network to do some astrophotography and take up the Messier Marathon again, painful as that would be without Maia's company. Nevertheless, I was able to capture some great shots using a remote telescope in Argentina. The experience rekindled my interest in meteors.

I had read about a recent meteorite strike in Antarctica. Investigation and study had been turned over to Chilean astronomers and scientists, many of whom I had met on my earlier world tour of the planet's observatories. On that trip, as astronomers do, I was able to take advantage of the hospitality and the telescopes of facilities and friends in the opposite hemisphere. I had fond memories of viewing the Southern Cross from Argentina, and a picture commemorating that event was displayed prominently in my office at home.

Last I had heard, my colleague astronomer Carlos Gonzales was stationed at the National Astronomical Observatory in Chile, so I sent a communication request, and he replied immediately, initiating a video chat. I inquired what he and his colleagues had learned from the meteorite's impact site.

He shook his head and cast his eyes down. When he looked up again, he said, "Sadly, all of the members of the investigation team contracted the virus and have died."

I was aghast. "I am so sorry to hear that, Carlos. My heart goes out to you."

Carlos said it would not be possible for him to visit the actual crater site, but he had something he wanted to show me. At the crash location, when all in the team were in good health, they had found an object that resembled an hourglass at the bottom of the crater. It was symmetrical and about five centimeters long and three centimeters wide at the top and bottom, and about one centimeter in diameter in its center. Surprisingly, it was very dense, weighing in at over 100 kilograms. It also appeared to have a magnetic field.

"We have not previously seen anything like this," Carlos said. "We're assuming it came in on or with the meteor, which must have burned up because we found no other space debris within three kilometers of the landing site other than this object." He estimated the strange artifact had been subjected to temperatures over 2,000 degrees Celsius upon entry to the atmosphere. "I am not sure what kind of alloy this thing is made of. I will send you a picture."

The image appeared on the screen of my communicator instantly. I had never seen anything like it. Its smooth exterior and designed appearance led me to believe it had been deliberately fashioned; it was not a random piece of space debris. It clearly represented an

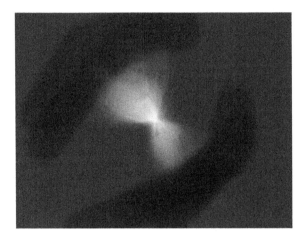

object from outer space, more than a broken part flung off a reentering satellite.

Carlos assured me that he would preserve the object and further analyze it when he could put together a study team, but there was little interest in space debris given the global health crisis.

And the pandemic did dominate the news media as stories poured in from all corners of the world. The data on infection rates and mortality were sobering. Society was shuttered, and the economy was in shambles. Fortunately, the food chain was still mostly intact, but there were fears that this was also in danger of collapsing.

Some, like my father-in-law and his sister, retreated to a remote location; they relocated to their mountain home upstate. Others consented to be microchipped to facilitate contact tracing and emergency information on the whereabouts of sick patients who entered a hospital alone and then disappeared into the system. I stayed put in the city, leading a spartan existence and spending most of my free time at the observatory. A return to outer space started to feel more and more enticing.

—

The media stories piled up, chronicling a new reality for a world struggling to cope with a lethal pandemic. Citizens around the world looked to their country's medical science professionals for protection against an illness that quickly claimed its victims. With the capacity of the medical infrastructure exceeded, and bodies accumulating, traditional methods of burial were abandoned. The corpses were considered infectious until cremated, and crematoriums were plunged into a logistical nightmare. Families might only receive their loved one's electronic medical record, with a death summary, then the trail ended upon cremation. A death certificate could be used to claim the cremated remains, which came in a generic container that resembled a two-pound coffee can from the old days. Even then, people wondered whether they were receiving their family member's genuine remains; rumors spread that the workers at the mortuaries were so overwhelmed that they filled the casks with ashes from a commingled pile of remains that exited the furnaces on a conveyor belt. Other dead were sterilized by irradiation, placed in aluminum caskets, and buried in huge municipal graveyards.

The experts recommended everyone stay home in a modified quarantine termed social distancing. All but essential services were closed; it was impossible to get a haircut or go to the gym. Going outside for a walk or exercise was allowed as long as everyone kept their distance from each other. Visitation with family and friends was discouraged.

Reality set in when parents requested grandparents not visit their grandchildren. The conundrum worsened as parents became increasingly fearful for their own lives. When the younger generation started to realize that they could inadvertently transmit the virus to their parents and potentially be responsible for "killing" Mom or Dad, it left them with disastrous angst. The pandemic marched across the globe.

For the most part, people were fearful of contracting the illness and abided by the governmental recommendations. But there were dissenting opinions, and some would not follow the rules as laid out by the chief scientists. The economy was in the throes of a recession, and there were talks of a depression. Interestingly, there seemed to be a big disconnection between the real world and the financial sector. Although the sky was falling and the economy was crashing, the financial experts continued to speculate and advise investors on how to capitalize on the situation and potentially make millions in a down economy.

Colleges and universities rearranged their curriculums to accommodate online studies. Theater and concert performances were canceled. Musicians and actors could be added to the list of unemployed. The airline industry was hobbled, save for a few flights. Most people were afraid to travel except for in the privacy of their own automobiles. People used hand sanitizer before and after pumping gas, visiting the ATM, and opening doors. Touching your face was not recommended; shaking hands and embracing in friendship or greeting were gone from the culture. Dating moved online — a kiss could be a death sentence. Occasionally, people would meet in a parking lot but remained in their cars to talk to each other. There was a lot of finger-pointing and accusations of incompetence in the government and world health agencies.

On a brighter note, freeway traffic congestion was greatly reduced. The brown cloud of air pollution dissipated. One could actually breathe the air, and many people rediscovered the beauty of the outdoors. Families were reunited as children returned home from lost jobs and shuttered schools. A new generation of babies emerged and later would be called "Covidians." The family barbecues, arts and crafts, puzzle making, and board games that had gone out of fashion returned. But this all came to an end as the second, third, and seemingly unending waves of infection marched onward.

The pandemic was greatly politicized, and elected officials played musical chairs trying to put forth an effective response without sufficient data. Similarly, people were considerably divided in their responses and opinions regarding this most unwelcome disruption to their lives. That is until someone close to them contracted a severe case of the illness. Only then would people grasp the gravity of the situation. Others, particularly the young and the healthy, frequently exhibited mild to moderate symptoms and so downplayed the situation.

Things changed when the scope of the problem became more evident and the country shut down. The economic impact of lost jobs and the inability to pay bills sharpened the developing crisis. The government poured money into the economy with increased unemployment benefits, direct aid, and loans. There was a mixed public response even as legislators debated the price tag. Some advocated fiscal restraint; others pushed for a more liberal position of helping everyone at any expense.

As the pandemic worsened, indiscriminately affecting all segments of the population, people started to panic. Efforts toward self-preservation and survival prevailed, and some rejected government interference in their lives.

Of the world's population of 10 billion people, so far, twenty percent had lost their lives, for a total of 2 billion souls. Wave after wave of infections crashed across society. The epidemiologists hoping for flattened curves and declining infection rates were instead met with a tsunami of unrelenting infections.

The Holy Grail became a vaccine. Public health and infectious disease experts championed the development of a vaccine coupled with preventative measures. With this one-two combo, they hoped to drive the virus into extinction, as had been done previously with the smallpox virus.

No matter, the world would be and already was permanently changed.

CHAPTER 8

Second Deployment

The world was such a mess. In many ways, I longed to return to the safety of outer space!

I made no progress locating Maia despite exhaustive efforts. I had reviewed all the recordings from every surveillance camera in the subway system, including street-level exits and the same with the art museum, but found nothing. Maia, it appeared, had literally disappeared. I visited my family, who were also in shock and disbelief, and I maintained a connection to Heather and Angelo even though public health mandates were urging citizens to curtail the number of interactions they had outside their household. I convinced Space Command of my fitness to return to the space station, and soon I would experience a new type of weightlessness, liberated not only from the gravity but also from the sadness of conditions on Earth.

Once settled on the space station, I began the work

of assembling and installing the new modules we carried in the cargo bay. It was exciting to upgrade the space station with the addition of new equipment. Through the communications channel, Maia and I had previously built, I could speak with Heather. I sent her some great pictures of the aurora as it looks from space. Curiously, she mentioned that the defibrillator business was booming because of a new epidemic of cardiac arrests, possibly a side effect of drugs people were taking in desperate attempts to prevent illness or viral infection of the heart directly. Oh my! An epidemic on top of a pandemic.

Some of the new equipment delivered to the space station was designed to monitor the heavens for potential communications from extraterrestrial life sources. We generally believed in the strong likelihood that intelligent life exists in the universe. Aboard the station, over many an evening meal, the crews from various nations discussed the rather complex Drake equation. Although it contained many theoretical variables, some no more than guesses, it allowed us to imagine a pathway toward locating ET life-forms. And if so, we believed, following the theorizing of our planet's highest minds, it was necessary to develop prime directives in preparation for such contact.

By virtue of my academic standing and training to become an astronaut, I had been invited to participate in the First Contact Committee. Potential issues included practical and philosophical ones. The assessment of danger could involve both. In addition to a space crew's physical and environmental needs, such as food, water, air, and life-support systems for extensive exploration, the committee carefully considered cultural concerns: Would both parties be sufficiently evolved to enter into a relationship with alien life-forms? Could we trust one another not to attempt to conquer, control, or exploit the other? The history of humankind has not been exactly exemplary in that regard. Our history is replete with disputes, armed conflict over land, resources, culture, and even race. At one point, the committee had posed the question: Is the pursuit of extraterrestrial life even in our best interest?

Rarely was the First Contact Committee able to rest on a definite answer to any of these questions. Despite all of the unknowns, the search for extraterrestrial life remained in the background as one of our crew's mission objectives.

I kept thinking back to my last deployment and brief viewing of a "spaceship" on that fateful day of Maia's disappearance. I had rationalized it as an illusion. And without further evidence, it was probably best to accept that because no one else on the station seems to have seen anything.

About a month after my return to the station, Ground Control pushed an alert concerning increased solar flare activity, which is often followed shortly thereafter by a tsunami of highly energetic particles and radiation.

My mouth went dry when I recalled the previous storm

on the day of Maia's disappearance. I briefly fantasized that perhaps I could somehow be swept away into the cosmos to join her wherever she had disappeared to. Soon the external detectors signaled the storm's arrival.

Returning to my observation window, I was astonished to once again see the spacecraft that lived only in my dreams. Was it an illusion or déjà vu? Suddenly, I felt very strange. I was dizzy and thought I might lose consciousness but then quickly regained clarity. I heard the voices of children.

CHAPTER 9

Childhood
Terminated

"Mister, Mister, can we have another ride? Can you make this thing go faster?"

I was surrounded by a crowd of children. They were banging on the windows and doors.

I appeared to be at an amusement park in the control room of a ride that appeared to be the main attraction.

My spacesuit was adorned with stars and lettering that echoed the words *Fantasy Adventure*, which was displayed on the marquee across the way. Another sign read *No Adults Allowed*.

Two young girls were at the head of the line for this ride. They were speaking simultaneously, interrupting each other, and giggling. One caught sight of me and said, "Hey! Where did you come from?"

"We want to go to Parents' World," they announced simultaneously.

"Yeah, we want to go put some parents in time-out for being so stupid," the second girl said, and they burst out laughing. "Where did you come from anyway? You sort of look like a parent," they queried.

"Oh, no, not me, you must be mistaken," I responded, playing along with them. "I am definitely not a parent."

"Yeah," said the first girl. "He's way too cool, look at his uniform."

"And he runs Adventure Land," said the second girl. They then launched into a dialogue between themselves, alternating among speaking, laughing, and giggling.

"Yeah, we want to go to Parents' World and find a few parents to wait on us. You know, the one where we could have anything we want, and the parents have to do what we say."

"Yeah, let's turn off their internet and make them do homework and talk to each other. We can change their passwords and get full access to the internet."

"Ooh! Or how about a family vacation and make them visit their cousins and grandparents?"

"Sure! And we can make them go to church!"

"Yeah! And clean up their rooms, walk the dogs, and change the litter boxes!" They burst out laughing again.

"Okay, put on these helmets and hop in," said a young male attendant who was standing next to me. He appeared to be around eighteen years old and handsome. After surveying me, head to toe, he asked, "Where *did* you come from? I don't recall seeing you before. And how old are you anyway?" Picking up his communicator, he spoke: "I stepped out of the control room to help some passengers, and this old guy appeared. I have never seen him before. His name tag says his name is William. I think he came out of the transporter. He is in uniform. I thought he was a new employee. Do you know anything about him?"

His supervisor arrived, politely introduced himself as Zach, and requested that we go to his office. Once inside, Zach introduced me to two other young men. "Can you tell us about yourself and explain why you are here?" he asked.

"Well," I began, finding myself nearly as bewildered as they looked. "I am an astronaut from the planet Earth," I responded. "I guess I was sent here?"

"That is very interesting," replied Zach. Turning to his two colleagues, he said, "Something must be wrong with the system. He is probably an anomaly and not real." He turned back to me. "We have never heard of a planet called Earth, so perhaps it would be best if you returned there."

"Wait a minute," I said. Confusion flashed across their faces. "I wouldn't be so hasty," I suggested. "Where are all the adults?"

"We are not familiar with the term 'minute,'" Zach said, with a questioning look. Then he continued, "We used to have adults and parents, but they have all died from the virus."

Whoa! A virus was devastating here, too, wherever

I was? "I am sorry to hear that. However, I assure you I am real, and I am an adult, and I have a background in coding. Therefore, this might be a good opportunity to troubleshoot your system," I suggested.

The three young men stepped out into the hallway, but I could hear them talking.

"Do you think he's the holographic engineer?" Zach asked.

"How would we know?" one of his companions replied. "We have never seen the engineer."

After further talk in muffled tones, they returned to the room, and Zach announced, "We are curious. Although we have never heard of Earth, we would like you to try to convince us you're real and establish your credibility."

They escorted me to an elevator, and we descended underground. We emerged in what appeared to be a control room or data center. "We will give you access to our database," Zach said. "Perhaps you can show us where this Planet Earth is."

Donning helmets and what looked like gamer gloves, we entered a virtual world. I asked to see a star chart and view of the solar system. With a few swipes, Zach gave me access to the astronomy database.

"I have never seen anything like this," I said. "How many planets are in your planetary system, and what is the distance to your sun? I will need access to telescope images." I gazed at the three-dimensional star chart. I was looking in from an unfamiliar perspective. I learned that there were only four planets in this particular system and that the one we were on was tidally locked, with a synchronized rotation and orbit, so that one side always faced the central star, which never moved in the sky, giving them constant daylight.

Zach explained that telescopes existed on the dark side of the planet, in the eternal darkness, but there was not a lot of interest in going over there because it was so cold and boring.

"Well, the universe is a big place," I said. "I might be able to show you where in the galaxy the planet Earth resides."

"How is it that you are able to operate our video interface if you're from another planet?" asked Zach.

I paused to consider. "Well, I would assume that there are inherent similarities in all control systems. We use similar technology on Earth." Interestingly, they actually had a fairly sophisticated astronomy database here. "I think there's a good chance I will be able to locate my home solar system, although this may take a while."

"How long do you need?" Zach asked.

"On Earth, we measure time based on the rotation of our planet, which takes twenty-four hours. I'll probably need one to two Earth days. However, a more scientific and less ambiguous metric is related to the vibrations of atoms in an atomic clock. What is your unit of time measurement?" I asked.

"We have never heard of hours or days. We use restoration units, which is the amount of time it takes our brains to reset. We have to do that regularly to avoid brain paralysis — when we are unable to think clearly, pay attention, or move about."

"Oh, I see. We have a similar need; we call it sleep," I replied.

"If you would continue your work, we will return in one restoration unit." Whereupon they exited the virtual room, leaving me to study the charts and information.

I hoped I could find my bearings. I really did not know where I was, but clearly in another planetary system. On Earth, our nearest neighbor star is Proxima Centauri about four light-years away. That was the minimum distance from home I could possibly be. No one would've had the opportunity to view our solar system, much less the Earth, from another vantage point, so none of this looked familiar.

I could only hope that I was at least in the same galaxy, where I might be able to recognize some constellations. Despite the almost incomprehensible distances, I reasoned, if I focused upon the more distant stars, the sky could theoretically look similar to a view from Earth or the space station.

Eventually, I was able to surmise that I was still within the Milky Way galaxy but probably farther out on one of the spiral arms. I might be able to find our sun, but locating the Earth would be like searching for an exoplanet.

While manipulating the controls, I was startled by the sudden appearance of a visitor. A shimmering apparition in the shape of a human materialized next to me.

"Greetings. I am the holographic engineer. What is the nature of your inquiry?" a female voice asked.

"I am William, from another planetary system and planet. I am trying to locate my home system on the star chart, as requested by Zach. I think he and his friends are currently in a restoration cycle," I responded.

She hesitated and appeared to be thinking. "You are clearly not from here," she responded. "What is the problem with the theme park?" she asked.

"I am not sure. We would have to wake up the attendants to answer that question."

"I am running diagnostics," she replied. "Yes, there appears to be a problem," she stated, "and your visitation has been expected, but I am unable to ascertain who sent you, although your presence computes."

She must have somehow come to the conclusion that I was not a threat or that I could at least be utilized to help her. She went on to teach me about the great viral pandemic that had overtaken this planet. A meteorite had struck the dark side of the planet, and within approximately 500 restoration units, an illness developed that was highly lethal to adults.

On the afflicted planet, the average life span had decreased to approximately 10,000 restorations, after which time most everyone died in their late twenties of the viral infection. As the older citizens categorically died off, those still alive recognized that the species faced potential extinction. As a final gift to their soon-to-be-orphaned children, they created and built this Adventure Land virtual system. The theme park experience included restorative learning sessions whereby the children — their childhood now terminated — could experience the trials of growth and maturation and assimilate the knowledge of these lessons into the wisdom of their premature adulthood. The last older generation had brilliantly devised what amounted to virtual parenting, which enabled them to preserve and pass on the brain trust of knowledge, experience, and wisdom to guide future generations.

I went on to learn that the holographic engineer was the executive director of this elaborate computer network. I was quite impressed with her abilities. She demonstrated advanced artificial intelligence. "You speak with a female voice," I said to her. "I'm curious. Do you have a name? And can you assume a physical form?"

"I was named after the code designer who created me. Her name was Radian," she replied. "I once had a body. They are useful at times but suffer from design and maintenance problems. As with the inhabitants of this planet, they are susceptible to many dangers essential for the perpetuation of the species. And to manipulate three-dimensional solid objects."

She continued: "My body has long since passed, and my essence was transferred into a quantum computer. Ironically, I may also require restoration someday."

Their computing technology was based on a sophisticated quantum device. The hardware was capable of representing a large number of possible states.

"I have detected a drive failure," Radian said. "This eventuality was anticipated; the drives can function for approximately five hundred of your Earth years before requiring maintenance."

"Does that mean this planet has been under siege by the virus for nearly half a millennium?" I asked.

"Yes," she said simply. "A notification has been posted stating that you were sent here to help. However, I am unable to verify its origin. Your presence is internally consistent. You will be granted access."

It turned out that restoration cycles were approximately twelve Earth hours. Once the attendants were awake, Radian announced that I was sent to show them how to repair, reinstall, and restart the theme park drive. We went down a long hallway that terminated at a large, heavy steel door. As we approached, the door opened, revealing a large room with three transparent cubes, each about the size of a deep freeze. They contained stacks of three toroidal objects.

A fourth unit was docked and connected to multiple wire harnesses. This one emitted a dim orange glow. Radian appeared as a sparkling figure of thousands of lights in the shape of a woman. She put on a bodysuit, which gave her a more tangible appearance. "This drive is demonstrating annihilation fatigue," she said. The three toroidal cores were storage rings containing entangled electrons and positrons, their ultimate state the result of calculations that would be observed and therefore determined in the third ring. "William, to accomplish our task, I will have to connect to your brain, and we will transiently share one mind. You will experience the universe through the lens of a different reality. The process will not be harmful to your physical form."

I was absolutely astounded by this technology. Radian explained that our task would be to connect and reboot from one of the spare drives. Then we needed to attach the spent drive to a linear accelerator to replenish it with electrons and positrons. With her guidance, the task consumed four restoration units.

The new drive now displayed three brilliantly illuminated rings that were rapidly changing colors. After restoration and sleep for myself, we returned to the surface to find the theme park once again operational. Throngs of youth looked forward to their adventure, unaware that they would soon leave their childhood behind and exit the ride as adults.

The next thing I knew, I was peering out of the space station window, face-to-face with a spaceship, its silhouette revealed by the storm of solar particles. Russ and Jim were sailing toward me across the gravity-free space, just exactly as they were before I landed in the Adventure Land park. It was as if not a millisecond had skipped. Did I really meet Zach and Radian and the kids on the parentless planet?

I struggled to understand what was happening to me. I glanced down. In my hand was a small communicator displaying the solar storm alert from Ground Control, and on my chest were emblazoned the words: "Fantasy Adventure Land! Come have the experience of your life!" I drew in a quick breath. Proof!

Russ reached out, and I handed him the communicator. He didn't seem to notice anything different about me, but I looked down again at the T-shirt I was wearing. It was like a souvenir that you'd wear home from a rock concert or a theme park — and it was, at minimum, a welcome testimonial that I had really somehow visited another planet.

Later, in my sleep sack, I connected to the station's network and checked the daily log. Sensors throughout the space station modules and pods documented my continual presence; the stream of data feeding back to Ground Control from my telemetry link was uninterrupted. The spaceship had vanished the moment before I turned away from the window, and the surveillance cameras had recorded nothing.

How could I explain my trip to Adventure Land? I had been there for what felt like many days. I decided I could not report my experience because it was theoretically impossible. A conversation I'd had with Maia long ago flashed across my mind. She had expressed concern about the potential ill effects of radiation while I was in space. Perhaps she was correct, and these hallucinations were symptoms of radiation poisoning?

But I was convinced my visit to Adventure Land was real. Nonetheless, I decided to increase my intake of antioxidants — free radical-scavenging medications — and started wearing a lead-lined hoodie to provide additional protection, although my space station colleagues said it was unnecessary.

Had I really made contact with an alien species?

CHAPTER 10

—

Virtual Perfection

D ay and night don't really exist in space. The periodic
alternation of sunlight and darkness associated with
orbiting a planet or a sun changes rapidly. The rhythms
I was used to on Earth were disrupted, to say the least.
To ameliorate the effects of disrupted biorhythms, the
engineers of the space station had created a surrogate
system that allowed us to alter the amount of light entering
through the windows and the intensity and color of
internal lighting.

Sleep researchers had discovered that by taking
advantage of our sensitivity to various colors and
wavelengths of light, a type of pseudo-circadian rhythm
can be established. The mission safety officer on Earth
monitoring our telemetry data had noted that I had not slept
for almost forty-eight hours. Concerned about the poor
outcomes of sleep deprivation, she prescribed a sedative.

I finally found myself getting sleepy and turned in for some rest. One would think that the weightlessness of space would be a great facilitator of rest and sleep, something that the mattress manufacturers on Earth could capitalize on. Imagine the advertisements: "Experience the unworldly feeling of sleeping in outer space," and the lines of insomniacs wanting that mattress. The weightlessness of space changed my perceptions of what a mattress should be. But, although considerable effort had gone into the design of my sleep sack, I never found anything better for sleep than my sleeping bag stretched out beneath the Montana sky and the hypnotizing effect of the stars and constellations.

In any event, the sleep medication proved quite effective, and soon I was resting in a deep sleep. Sometimes medication can produce some spectacular side effects and bizarre behaviors. I thought I was dreaming, but everything was so vivid and real. I wondered what would happen if I could no longer tell the difference between dream and reality.

I found myself walking around a fountain in a town square. The temperature was pleasant; two suns, one large, one small, shone down from the sky above. Green grasses and colorful flowers and gnarled trees and magnificent sculpted gardens flourished in every direction.

A uniformed officer approached and said, "You are in violation of Statute 34.7 section D and 689.23 section

T(z). You are under arrest." Handing me a face mask, he continued, "Breath through this. You must go to quarantine." A truck with *Decontamination Unit* stenciled on the doors pulled up.

"Wait a minute! I can explain!" I said quickly.

"This is not harmful. Just comply," the man replied. He and the driver sprayed me with a warm foam that actually felt pretty comfortable before it started to harden. With me immobilized, they replaced the face mask with a helmet and bulky suit and placed me in the back of the truck.

We drove for about fifteen minutes in what appeared to be a silent electric vehicle. Oddly, we entered a roundabout, drove around in a clockwise direction, circled twice, then exited onto a driveway that led to a large building. The groundskeepers were busily attending to the absolutely spotless sidewalks and perfectly manicured gardens. I was placed in a motorized cart and wheeled to the entrance.

Once inside the building, we encountered a security team that directed us to the decontamination center. The suit and helmet were connected to hoses, and I could feel warm air pumping in. Then I was taken before a panel of seven men and women for questioning.

The arresting officer read the charges: violation of ordinances 100-A, 202-B, and 303-C of Statute 34.7, and 404-D and 505-E of Statute 689.23. As far as I could tell, they were accusing me of loitering, vagrancy, failure to possess identification, failure to possess and use viral protection equipment, and walking against the flow of traffic. The good news was that I tested negative for viral particles. They wheeled me to a windowless room that was nevertheless pleasantly lit, and I fell asleep.

I was tested a second and third time twelve hours apart to achieve a ninety-nine percent true negative status, after which I was delivered from the suit and polymer decontamination cocoon. Once removed, I was given clothing and accommodations courtesy of the state.

A representative of the state was scheduled to meet with me the following day.

The room they put me in was spacious and a nice break from the cramped quarters of the space station. I was being held captive, but the quarters had nutrition and sanitization stations, and I was perfectly comfortable and quite well-rested. The food was like typical space station fare, nutritious, low-residue, and good for you.

After a night's sleep, I cleaned up and put on the set of fresh clothing that had arrived by drone in preparation for the day's events. A chime sounded, and I opened the door.

A young woman was there. "Hello, my name is Virtually Perfect," she said. "I have been assigned to assist you." She appeared to be human, although her shoulder-length blonde hair did partly obscure her pointed ears. She was relatively tall, slender, and sharply dressed in a dark pantsuit and polished shoes. She had five fingers on each hand, and her nails were well manicured; the painted color matched her pink lipstick. Overall, she appeared humanoid.

"Please follow me, William. Please wear your mask and maintain a three-meter distance," she said.

Exiting the room, we entered a parade of people, each spaced three meters from the next. The walls of the corridor were a clear glass-type material, and I could see that everyone was walking only in a clockwise direction around a central atrium. People lined up at circular hand-washing stations, and each individual diligently scrubbed their hands. Ms. Perfect joined a line, so I followed her, maintaining a three-meter distance. The soap dispensers rhythmically delivered precisely five milliliters of cleanser, and timers accurately designated a sixty-second wash period followed by fifteen seconds of rinsing. Then we each moved to a drying station and on to an emollient dispenser where I saw others disappear behind closed doors. But Ms. Perfect merged into traffic, and we walked onward.

Apparently, right turns and backtracking were not allowed. After we arrived, I noticed that our destination was the next door to the right from my room, and we had circumnavigated the entire complex to arrive at the adjacent room.

"All right, Mr. Williams, let's get started," she said.

I smiled at her. "My first name is William," I said, holding out my hand.

She looked up from her tablet, blinked at me, and

returned her gaze to the electronic documentation before her. "We will need to fill out these forms in preparation for your hearing. What is your full name? What is the time, date, and location of your birth?"

"I am William Preston. I was born on March 2, 1985, at midnight in Missoula, Montana. The United States of America on the planet Earth."

She raised her eyes to mine again and blinked in confusion. "Are you certain? I have never heard of such times or places. Let me remind you, if you fail to cooperate with the approved process, there will be consequences. The situation will get complicated. Let us try another approach. How did you come to be breaking multiple longstanding regulations, and on the town square no less? How did you get there?" she asked a little less sternly.

"Well, Ms. Perfect, you may not believe me, but I am an astronaut, and I am not certain as to my purpose here. I believe I was sent here."

"Unfortunately, none of those answers fit the form format. Neither are they believable or compatible with established protocol," she said. She let out a sigh. "We will have to default to a narrative presentation. Just know that, depending on the presiding official, there is little tolerance for such nonuniform situations. You could be declared indigent and in need of mental evaluation, after which I may not be able to help you."

"Sometimes, Ms. Perfect, it is necessary to look beyond

what seems to be the immediate data to understand a situation."

She seemed puzzled by that but gamely pressed on. "All right, I will attempt to do so. Let us proceed to record your narrative."

"Tell me about yourself," I asked instead.

"This is not about me," she replied, again blinking prettily.

"Well, then, can you at least tell me about this world? What is the name of this planet? And how long have you struggled to contain the virus?"

"A better question would be: How could an indigent spaceman who does not even know his own birthdate or place know anything about a virus?" she replied indignantly.

I noticed that she was even prettier when she was agitated. Then I noticed that I noticed. I forced my mind back to the issue at hand. "Did your planet experience a meteorite impact?" I asked.

"Again, this discussion is about you."

"Well, I guess we are experiencing a virtually perfect standstill," I replied.

"Ha, ha, very funny." But a smile cracked through. "You know, I could have you committed, and then you could tell your jokes to the other comedians who failed to see the gravity of their situation," she concluded with a grin.

"I wondered if you had a sense of humor." I laughed

with her. "Tell me about the pandemic."

She stared at me, her smile fading into a frown. A single tear appeared in the corner of her brown eyes. "Well, okay. You're right. We were hit by a meteor, and about a year after the strike, people in the surrounding area became ill with a mysterious but deadly ailment. Shortly thereafter, the alarm went out about a new, highly lethal infectious disease. Historically, we had been devastated by many infectious disease outbreaks, so our society is one that values preparation and standards above all else."

I nodded. This planet's fate sounded like a familiar trajectory.

"We knew what must occur. The Chief Bureaucrat ordered our planetary crisis laws, policies, and procedures in effect. An immediate quarantine was established. We'd been able to isolate a contagion into extinction before. Everyone was provided with automated shipments of supplies and medicines so they wouldn't have to leave their residences."

"Seriously? How could you enforce such draconian measures?" I asked.

She looked at me skeptically. "We all recognized that lives would be saved in the long term. Unfortunately, this viral agent proved highly lethal and resistant to our crisis management procedures."

I nodded, and she continued.

"I was spared by virtue of my work here. One morning,

travel in and out of my home region was shut down, so I had to say my goodbyes to my family electronically from work. I never got to go home again. Within a few months, everyone there had perished, including my husband and two children. At this point, the entire region remains abandoned and under tight quarantine and surveillance."

She was one very resilient and strong person. What a horror it is to be cut off from your family forever in the course of a day. I was still mourning the loss of one person, Maia. I couldn't imagine how sorrowful and lost Virtually Perfect must have felt.

She paced around the room but never strayed less than three meters away from me and continued the dialogue. "We are a disciplined culture, and we understand the need for strict adherence to rules and protocol. We socially isolate; we wash our hands; we wear personal protective garments and respirators. Disinfection is the norm and the rule. We travel unidirectionally in buildings and on roads and sidewalks — as you discovered. You were walking in the wrong direction. Right-hand turns are illegal. Restaurants, theaters, and community gatherings are a way of the past. The crisis laws, I fear, will be in effect indefinitely into the future."

A shiver ran down my spine. I couldn't imagine existing long-term in such an austere atmosphere. Is this where Earth was headed?

"We continue to get all our food and deliveries via

self-steering drones and vehicles. We have nano-implants for identification and to make financial transactions easier, although the bureaucracy covers everyone's universal expenses, so there is hardly a need for financial accounting. I noticed that you are missing your ID chip. It is illegal to remove them, you know."

"We do not have such implants where I come from," I replied.

"Do you really expect me to believe that you are some off-planet being? Even if that were the case, the odds of us meeting are at least one in a trillion," she said.

She must have been familiar with some version of the Drake equation! If she knew the odds, then her culture surely must have at some point considered the existence of "alien" life forms in the star systems beyond their planet's. "Ms. Perfect," I said excitedly. "Yes, I am from a different planet, a different star system — the solar system, we call it — and maybe even a different time." I had started to consider the time factor in my otherworldly excursions because it seemed like my time away did not register in my personal timeline and that perhaps I was traveling to these planets at different times in their evolution so I could put together the pieces of their story in some fashion that would help the Earth.

She was shaking her head. She sat down across from me. I noticed she disregarded the minimum spacing rule. Her soft brown eyes filled with worry. "No, that is impossible. And that is why you are a threat to our survival," she said, suddenly pounding her fist upon the table between us. "You're an unknown quantity. Unregulated. You don't fit in. You're not following the rules. We are the preppers. We understand discipline and value preparedness." Her hand flung up to her chest. "*I* won the Citizens Preparatory Award in college, and that's when they changed my name. I was not always Virtually Perfect. After I became separated from my former life, I was given this job, a new identity, and a chance to start over, to live up to my name."

"Wow, I am sincerely sorry." I inched my hand closer to hers across the table. "That is hard to comprehend. It would be very difficult. My life also suddenly changed when I wasn't prepared. Nothing has been the same since. That day, my wife disappeared without a trace, and then our planet succumbed to a terrible viral pandemic, just like yours. I returned to space to escape it all, and I currently live in a space station." I paused and looked deeply into her eyes. She returned my gaze steadily. "Something is going on with this virus that decimates a population and ends up changing the whole civilization, but I am not sure what. I would agree with you that an unknown agent can be dangerous. However, my appearance here on your planet is my second such excursion to another planet that defies the known laws of physics. Try to calculate those odds! It cannot be accidental."

She looked somewhat calmer, and her expression had softened.

"Let me tell you about Earth, and Montana, my favorite place," I said, hoping to ease any remaining tension she might be feeling. I gave her a summary of ranch life in Montana and growing up knowing I would become an astronaut someday, meeting Maia, heading into space, losing Maia, and finally returning to space and having these unusual adventures I'd been cast into.

"Well, that is quite a story," she said, busily documenting every word. "Off the record, from one orphan to another, I am also sorry for your losses. I can partially understand. This is highly unusual." She looked me squarely in the eyes, all bureaucratic pretense dropped. "You realize this situation is impossible, correct?" Staring at me, she smiled and, with the monumental courage of the obsessive-compulsive, Virtually Perfect removed her mask and gloves, applied a hand gel, and then reached out to hold my hand.

We gazed at one another, and after a moment, she said, "We are not allowed to touch one another without a license. But for you, I would gladly do that and more."

Warmth rushed up and filled me inside. I squeezed her fingers and said, "I wish I could stay here with you. But my fate is unknown and not my choice right now. Otherwise, I would. You know," I said flirtatiously, "I would also change your name to 'Completely Perfect.'"

She gasped with laughter and grasped my hand even tighter. We both understood that this fleeting moment would be our last together.

Images of the interior of the space station spliced into my perception. I knew I would have to say goodbye quickly. I walked around the table and embraced Ms. Perfect. Then we shared the most impossible but precious kiss the universe could ever produce.

"Goodbye, William from Montana. I will always remember you."

When I awoke in my sleep sack, her scent remained. The reflective screen on my communicator showed pink lipstick rimming my lips. The dampness of my hands slowly evaporated, unlike the memory of Ms. Perfect and the prepper planet.

I sat in silence, contemplating the experience. That was no dream.

I had now seen the alien spacecraft three times and had been transported across the universe twice to separate and distinct planetary systems that contained intelligent life. The commonality of each experience seemed to be a meteor strike followed by a viral pandemic, and now that was exactly happening on Earth!

CHAPTER 11

Station Break

Work around the space station occupied me over the next few weeks. However, I was able to work on some of my own astronomy projects — searching for meteors and exoplanets.

One day, while pushing through a linkage tunnel to another part of the space station, my hand slapped down on an automatic external defibrillator, and I immediately thought of Maia. Later that day, I called Heather. We had not spoken for a while, and I was looking forward to catching up and hearing what was going on back in New York City. The first thing she told me was that she and Angelo were getting married. I offered hearty congratulations and let her know I was overjoyed for them. She also apprised me of the fact that she was in the process of starting an electronics business that would manufacture defibrillators. Apparently, worldwide demand for them was up, mirroring the rising cardiovascular complications of the viral infection, which had been named COVID.

"It's bizarre," she said, "having worked on the devices previously at VDM and then with what happened to Maia, and now we are thinking about manufacturing them. How ironic that these devices have become so intertwined in our lives," she said. "In a sense, I guess we owe it all to Maia."

Otherwise, things were not good on Earth. The virus was mutating, limiting the effectiveness of the vaccine that had been designed. The government of Workman and Cole was pushing economic relief legislation for the unemployed and failing businesses. Heather ended our call by saying that at least I was safe in the space station.

I was thinking about home and wondered about my family and friends and promised myself I would visit them all when I returned home at the end of this deployment.

—

CHAPTER 12

Eyes in the Backs of
Their Heads: The Janusians

Only one person was allowed outside the space station at a time, per regulations. Today that person was me. I was donning a spacesuit, preparing to venture out to work on a malfunctioning solar panel. As I stepped into the suit, with Jim's assistance, I started seeing lights, and the voices of my colleagues slowed to a stop as if time had paused.

I was disoriented for a moment but then regained my bearings. I was standing in another place surrounded by windows in what looked to be an observation platform. Out the far windows, I could see the space station with the Earth in the background.

An amorphous ball of light hovered in the room. A voice called out: "We are the Janus. Do not be afraid. We intend no harm."

I was unable to localize the source of the voice because

it appeared to be coming from within my head. "I am William from the planet Earth," I responded out loud. "We," I said, indicating myself and then gesturing toward the space station, "also wish you no harm."

"We are agents of the Klabyau in pursuit of Fermion, an intergalactic villain and thief. He is wanted for spreading contagion and plundering the universe."

Contagion! Were the Janus revealing the source of the viral agent?

The voice inside my head continued: "We will stop at nothing to put an end to his nefarious activity and recover the galaxy of the eleventh dimension that he stole from the Klabyau."

"I see," I said. "How may I be of assistance?"

"You undoubtedly recall our first encounter through the window of your space station? That was not a chance encounter. We had detected the characteristic signal of quantum universe shifting emanating from Earth and were investigating."

"Yes," I replied. "I have tried to rationalize that encounter as an anomaly of the solar storm. That date and event are indelibly etched in my memory. That is the date of my wife's mysterious disappearance and a great deal of chaos on Earth and in the space station resulting from the storm."

"Yes, that is correct," the voice said. "Given the continued detection of those signals, we were compelled to investigate. Since then, there has been a tremendous increase in the number of quantum shifting signals emanating not only from Earth but also from other planets throughout the galaxy. We believe them to be the trail left by Fermion."

I was astonished. They truly were tailing a suspect who traversed the universe.

"He travels in a small device known as a horizon modulator. When stationary, it appears as a white hourglass-shaped object. Once in transit, however, it becomes invisibly black, absorbing all light and gravity."

My fellow astronomer Carlos's space object sprang to mind.

"The horizon modulator contains the stolen eleventh-dimensional galaxy that can convey the gravitational force. Fermion has stolen the entire galaxy. The simultaneous occupation of multiple dimensions can be used for nefarious purposes to perpetrate evil, is antithetical to our beliefs, and is forbidden by intergalactic code."

There was an established intergalactic code? Thinking back to my training and participation on the First Contact Committee, I was encouraged by these remarks, which indicated I was dealing with an advanced, principled ET life-form. They seemed way ahead of us, in fact.

"Fermion is using the horizon modulator to spread disease throughout the universe in an attempt to conquer and obtain new worlds for exploitation. A contagion that lives in such a realm has proven most difficult to control and eradicate."

My heart sank. Fermion had released a resistant virus that was already decimating the Earth and was possibly incurable.

The voice inside my head continued: "There is only adaptation given a long enough trajectory in the fourth dimension. We have sent you throughout the universe — the Milky Way galaxy, to be more precise — as our proxy in search of Fermion. You may recall those events in your dreams. In order not to disturb the timeline or interfere with other civilizations, we have rules of engagement to guide possible encounters with other beings and civilizations. We intended to erase those memories from your brain and apologize for using you in that way."

"Wow! I thought those were dreams until I once returned wearing foreign clothing. Our civilization also has specific rules of engagement in the event of contact with extraterrestrial life," I responded. "I believe this to be a first encounter. I am honored to have this opportunity and welcome further dialogue. Please tell me more about yourselves and your purpose —and mine — for being here."

What sounded like a blended chorus of voices intoned the following information: "We are the Janus. We hail from the edge of the universe, where dark meets light. We exist in the border space between the light side and the dark. We face both directions and can see all.

"We are decedents of Source, which gives us the knowledge and ability to quantum shift and move about the universe. Your culture subscribes to the belief in a higher being or God, does it not?"

The voices paused, giving me a moment to think, and then resumed: "That is probably the closest analogy we can provide. As stated earlier, we detected the frequency signature of quantum dimensional shifting on the date of our first encounter with you. The first signal appears to have emanated from a location on Earth you designate as New York City."

For some reason, my mind immediately leaped to Maia, and I wondered whether the dimensional shifting signals had something to do with her disappearance on that same date and, out of all the possible places in the universe, from the location the Janus had pinpointed. "I think I can help find your missing universe," I spoke out loud, though I doubted I needed to vocalize because I could feel the presence of the Janus pulsing inside my mind. But I continued to speak and stare out the windows toward the distant image of the beautiful blue, green, and swirling white planet. "I know of such an object that you've described as the horizon modulator. I also have a great need to understand the events of the day of our first encounter when my wife vanished in New York City."

"If the disappearance of your wife is related to the dimension shifting we are detecting, that could only be the doings of the Source. No other entity in this galaxy has such ability."

I shook my head. Were they saying that Maia had been shifted by a higher power into another dimension?

"The rate of signals emitted from the planet Earth is increasing and remains to be explained. Would you accept our assistance in locating your wife in exchange for your information related to Fermion and the missing eleventh-dimensional galaxy of the Klabyau?"

"Yes, gladly. How shall we proceed?" I asked.

"We will set up a gravity portal and must act quickly because Fermion will be planning an escape. He has learned how to use the eleventh-dimensional galaxy to convey the force of gravity, and soon he may be able to escape on a gravity wave. We will return you to your space station and make preparations."

My foot slid down the pant leg of my spacesuit. Not a millisecond had passed, and Jim's voice replaced the voice of the Janus in my head:

"Let's go over the safety checklist," he said, "and then initiate decompression."

We systematically checked the items one by one. The value of doing so soon became apparent, as my thoughts were elsewhere. My mind was racing, trying to process all these developments while preparing for my upcoming spacewalk.

Any one of them alone would have been a monumental

discovery. I had just made contact with some serious extraterrestrial beings, who potentially had answers to some of the fundamental questions of physics, astronomy, and cosmology. Holy moly! I forced my mind back to the task at hand, promising myself I'd process this, put things into perspective, plan potential next moves, and develop a strategy later, in the privacy of my sleep sack.

I struggled with the idea of informing Space Command of my discoveries. My second deployment was drawing to a close and would be completed in a few weeks. A return to Earth seemed timely.

The next time the space station swung into alignment with the Southern Hemisphere, I contacted Carlos Gonzales in Argentina and arranged a visit a few weeks hence. It would be great to see him, and I told him I had information concerning his mystery object.

CHAPTER 13

—

Shaman

"Mayday! Mayday!" squawked from the speaker overhead. "This is Mundus Airlines flight one-two-two-niner requesting emergency assistance!"

I was standing straddling a carpeted aisle between rows of airplane seats, bracing my forearms against the overhead compartments. I appeared to be a flight attendant upon a stricken aircraft. I charged toward the cockpit and found the door unlocked, so I went in. There, I learned that the jet had just reached altitude and cruising speed when all the engines failed. They were able to restart the starboard engine, but it was faltering. They had restarted it twice, but it was not producing much power. The captain could raise no response from air traffic control. He pointed out a midsized airport on the chart that we might be able to use for an emergency landing.

Here we go again, I thought. These "excursions" were

getting increasingly dangerous. I half hoped this one was indeed only a dream.

"I have some flight experience," I said to the captain, who looked at me in bewilderment. I took out my communicator. "I need some data to make the calculations. It's a problem of calculating the kinetic energy of the aircraft and parlaying it into a flight plan," I said.

"I know that," said the captain. "However, there is no response from air traffic control. We will have to make the calculations ourselves."

"Yes, that's what I am saying." I tried to remain calm as the captain fine-tuned the controls in an attempt to pilot the falling mass of metal as a glider. "I would estimate we could probably 'glide' for about thirty to forty minutes and cover up to 200 miles, possibly farther, with partial power from the remaining engine. Please tell me our location, the mass of the aircraft, and its speed and altitude, and then distance and coordinates of the target airport."

"Who are you?" the captain asked.

"Think of me as a visiting astronaut," I said. "Coordinates, please."

"Visiting from where?"

"I am deployed to the space station orbiting the planet Earth. I have also been deployed to some other strange places recently, but we can discuss all that later. If we don't act now, we will all perish on this aircraft!"

The captain called out the parameters, which I repeated

into my communicator. A second later, the results were ready. "Here is the calculated flight plan. Follow it precisely. We will be landing at high speed." As an aside, I said, "Hopefully, the runway is long enough."

"Can you connect your device with this?" asked the captain, handing me what looked like a USB 1.0 cable. Staring at it, I realized I might be on Earth because where else would you find a connector like this? Unless USB was truly living up to its name as universal! I plugged in my communicator, and the flight plan appeared on the captain's control panel screen.

After reviewing the flight plan, the pilot and copilot concluded it was reasonable. "All right," said the captain. "Perhaps you should inform the passengers," he said to me. "What is your name again?"

"William. William Preston, at your service, sir," I said.

"I certainly hope so, William 'from Earth,'" he responded with a note of incredulity in his voice beneath the stress.

Maybe this wasn't Earth after all. But all the objects, people, language, and technology seemed familiar, Earth-like circa the 1990s. I returned to the main cabin as instructed and addressed the passengers over the PA. "Ladies and gentlemen, the captain has informed me that we have a critical situation. We have lost power to the engines. The good news is we are at altitude and high speed. We should be able to coast in for a landing. Please remain calm and prepare for an emergency landing."

Pandemonium erupted, but I spoke over the din: "We will be coming in fast, and things could get rough. Try to remain calm, please. Be sure to review the emergency landing information in your seatback pocket. I will update you shortly." I clicked off the intercom and scrambled back up to the cockpit to see if there was a place for me to strap in. The remaining engine was now completely unresponsive, but fortunately, the emergency power turbine was deployed, providing the captain with some control.

As we dropped in altitude, we were traveling quite fast. Finally, and still moving at a high rate of speed, we came in on the final approach knowing there would be no second chances.

The captain set down the wheels perfectly on the near end of the runway and applied the brakes. We could hear and feel the brakes engage with a familiar rumble and vibration.

When will we slow down? I thought, gripping my harness with both hands. The runway seemed to go on forever; however, we soon reached the end, and the plane exited onto the dirt — thankfully at a greatly reduced speed. The landing gear did not take the rough well and collapsed, so we slid in for a belly landing.

We could hear the passengers in panic mode. Though belted in, we were tossed around violently. It could have been a lot worse. When the plane groaned to a halt, everyone breathed a sigh of relief, followed by pandemonium again as passengers rushed the exits. So eager to get off the plane, they jumped onto the already-deployed evacuation slides. Except for the trauma of the near-death experience, it didn't seem like there were injuries beyond cuts, abrasions, and bruises.

I unbuckled quickly, stole out of the cockpit, and leaped to the ground. A grassy field stretched toward high wire fencing under a pale blue sky. It still seemed Earth-like, but there was something off about the overly white sunlight slanting down.

Once out in the field, I spotted an open suitcase, its contents somewhat scattered about. A jacket fit me perfectly and concealed my airline host's uniform.

Inside the terminal, I slipped into the crowd and evaded the minimal security, joining the flow of those exiting. The airport was eerily empty; hardly anyone was at this transportation center. I wasn't sure I was on Earth, given my conversation with the pilot. Perhaps this was another planet where the virus had adversely affected the normal comings and goings of the population, too. Once outside, I thought a guide would have been helpful, a Radian or Ms. Perfect perhaps. I reached inside the jacket pockets and found tickets and a passport belonging to a Mr. Louis McKay. He must be the key. I must have to find him.

Looking around, I discovered a rack of bicycles. Riding a bicycle was not my first choice; however, they were unlocked. The temptation was too great, so I selected one and rode off. The streets were devoid of cars and foot traffic, so I ventured out and rode down the centerline. Suddenly, a car came out of nowhere. Although we both tried to stop, I broadsided the vehicle and flew over the hood. Fortunately, the landing was on a patch of grass.

A woman approached. "You all right?" she asked.

"I think so," I said, picking myself up and brushing off. I looked at the woman, who was dressed in the styles of pants and blouse I had seen women wearing when we went into town for a night out when I was a kid in Montana. "Could you tell me what planet this is?" I asked.

"Oh, darn it all! You hit your head, didn't you?" she replied. "I'm so sorry. A man on a bike was the last thing I expected to encounter on these roads. Why don't you come sit down on this rock, hon," she said, patting a flat boulder that squatted in the middle of the grass. "Looks like your bike did not farewell. But I can give you a ride. Where are you going?"

I really felt fine and waved off the seat. "I am looking for a man at this address." I showed her the passport.

"Wow. That's far away, in the mountains. Probably a good place to hide out if you could find accommodations." She continued, "I can't take you there. It's too far, and I don't venture up there where the hard-core survivalists live. But I do volunteer at a shelter here in town. Why don't you come with me? Perhaps we might find you a ride to North County there. It's the least I could do for trashing your bike. Thank goodness you were not hurt," she said, placing a hand to her chest.

"I see," I said. "And what are those survivalists trying to survive?" She looked at me with sympathy for the apparent mind troubles I was having. "The pandemic."

The shelter looked to have been a blessing for the homeless during the plague. It represented their only option for food and a respite from the chaos. Everyone was fairly streetwise; social distancing came easily, and most wanted to be left alone anyway. Once dinner was over, the masks went back on, and people moved a bit closer to one another. The snippets of conversations I overheard were mostly about surviving — where to find the next meal and good places to stay.

The shelter was run by a local minister. He was very personable and was making his rounds, talking and checking in with everyone. When he came up to me, he said, "I have not seen you here before," holding out his elbow for a bump. "What brings you around, beyond the obvious, son?"

"I'm trying to find a man in North County."

"That's interesting," he said. "Not many people up in North County any longer, but I know a few folks there. What is this man's name?"

"Louis McKay," I replied.

"You're kidding!" The pastor slapped his thigh. "I

know him! I know him well. We go back a long way, probably forty years now. Lou and I started one of the first shelters in Atlantis together. We were in our twenties and on a mission to save the world — and we're still trying! I have not seen him for a while, but I'm sure he's at his place up north."

"Well, I need to talk to him. I have some papers that belong to him."

"I see," the pastor replied. "I may know someone going up that way. Let me see if I can find them."

"Thank you, sir," I said. "Much appreciated."

Later that evening, from a safe distance, I chatted with a woman whose daughter lived in North County. "What's the best way to get there?" I asked.

"There used to be a shuttle service, but I dunno if they're still in business."

I hoped the pastor would come through with a ride for me. The shelter provided blankets and a pad to soften the wooden floor. But it was summer and warm, so I chose to sleep outside on the lawn out back.

The next day, we all had coffee and oatmeal with toast for breakfast. A man approached me and said, "I hear you're trying to find Louis. I am taking some supplies to a church up there. I could get you to the general area."

"That would be great," I said. "I know his address."

It took the better part of the morning to get there. The man dropped me off in a steep valley containing a large lake at the foot of a mountain. He stopped the truck just where the road started to disintegrate. It looked like nature was reclaiming the roadway, and it had become impassable where it exited the valley to the north. The driver told me Louis's place was up there, another five kilometers or so.

It was warm and sunny, and the scenery looked familiar, just like the Montana of my youth. The sunlight warming my back was mild and colorless, casting the landscape into abnormally vivid relief. I started hiking, and after about an hour, I spotted what appeared to be the remnants of a group of cabins and a few homes, all long abandoned. A slightly concealed driveway led into the forest. A tree at the entrance displayed a worn address sign that read: 64575.

Not much remained. The home had collapsed into a pile of rotting logs. Curiously, in the yard nearby stood large rusting metal sculptures of an elk and a bison and a pair of tall cactus plants. I had to be getting close; the grass was trampled, and a dog's chew toys were scattered about.

Nearby, another home was in visibly better shape than the first. On the hillside, a pair of vertical flags beat in the wind. About a hundred meters farther in, an obscure entrance was overgrown with brush and trees. The sign said Go Away. I nervously entered, and shortly two dogs came running toward me, sounding the alarm. I remained calm. The black one busily sniffed me up and down and then marked an adjacent bush, gladly not my leg. The white one ran up the hill and returned accompanied by a man sporting a black-and-white braided beard and carrying a rifle. He approached cautiously. "What can I do for you?" he called from a good distance.

"Hello!" I called back. "I was on the plane and found a passport. I am returning it. Are you Louis McKay?"

"I might be. What plane?" he asked.

"You know, the one that came in hot, skidding on its belly."

"Oh, that one," he said, nodding. "That was a close call. I haven't traveled since, been over a year now. Were you also on the flight?" he asked.

"Why, yes, but it was only a few days ago, wasn't it?"

"Probably time dilation," he said, coming closer. "You might want to check those dates," he said, indicating the expired tickets I held in my hands.

Pausing, I looked at the tickets and was nearly speechless. It appeared that a year had passed since the crash landing. Time dilation?

"Sorry for the gun," Louis said. "Things are not the same given the pandemic. It's really just a deterrent, and I hope not to ever need it. Hey, thanks for returning this. What's your name?" he asked.

"William. William Preston," I said, extending my hand.

He shook it with no hesitation and clapped me on the shoulder. "Glad to meet you, William," he replied.

I removed his jacket and handed it to him. His eyes roamed over my airline uniform.

"Wait a minute, you're the missing person they were looking for, aren't you? You saved everyone! I wouldn't be here today if it were not for you." Louis clapped me on the shoulder again, put his arm around me, and escorted me up the driveway. "C'mon, we need to talk. Come inside. Let's have a drink."

I learned that Louis was a minister. When I told him I was an astronaut from another planet, he looked at me and said, "That's interesting. Which planet might that be? I've always wondered if there was intelligent life out there," he said, "but did not think it would be in this star system."

"I grew up on a planet named Earth in a solar system in the Milky Way galaxy."

He frowned, considering. "Nope, never hear of it."

He handed me a rocks glass half full of an amber liquid. "I guess an astronaut would be able to fly a plane. That makes sense. I have three questions for you: How did you get on the plane? Where have you been this last year? And what is your purpose here?"

"I'm not entirely sure about any of it," I replied. "I believe I was sent here as a proxy for those in pursuit of an outlaw of the universe who is spreading a virus around the galaxies."

"Under what authority do those in pursuit of this criminal operate?" he asked.

"They told me 'a higher power'? They are the Janus," I said.

Hesitating briefly, the expression on his face changed. "Are you serious?" he said.

"Do you know of them?" I asked.

"Yes, I do. I lived among them when I was younger. That did not go well. But we eventually came to an understanding. I continually ran afoul of their culture and beliefs. I needed to know more about everything back then than they were willing to show underlings. I reached a point where I wanted more freedom, which was not compatible with the life they envisioned for me. Had I stayed, I might have become a high priest by now," he mused. "But I had my own ideas on achieving enlightenment. Tell me more of this fugitive," he asked.

"Apparently, his name is Fermion, and he stole a galaxy. Reportedly he travels around the universe in some type of container masquerading as a meteorite, and then this plague follows in his wake."

"Well, this Fermion must be pretty slick. It's near impossible to remain concealed from the Janus," Louis said. "They 'see' almost everything, with a view toward the light and the dark sides of the universe. And that makes sense — because they're unable to easily assume a physical form. They would need your help to function beyond their realm. I chose to keep mine — my physical form, that is — and to remain here. This is a very unique place," he said. "There is a lot of energy passing through here. About 100 meters from here, in the draw, up between those cabins, lies a node of energy. There are several in the region that are focused on that peak," he said, pointing to an impressive cone-shaped mountain nearby.

We went outside again and walked past the spruce and pine into a forest of dense aspen trees. Although the air temperature felt like midsummer, the leaves were the most brilliant yellow imaginable. When we entered the grove, everything — our bodies and even the air — was enveloped by the warmth of pure yellow energy. We remained in the warm and peaceful yellow light, "sunbathing" and talking.

"What is this place?" I asked.

"I call it 'the clarifier,'" he responded. "It is a great place to hang out and meditate." We were sitting on a fallen log in the glade. Louis turned toward me and said, "It's starting to make sense now. I once knew a Fermion. We both trained with the Janus long ago. He stayed with them, whereas I came home here. I was surprised they accepted him into their order because it was known that he struggled with anger from a dark past."

He went on: "I would say your fugitive has definitely been here. There was indeed a meteor strike several years ago. I have seen the site out in the forest. Unimaginable destruction leveled everything for miles as if God had taken a deep breath and blew it all down," he said. "The viral pandemic started soon after. We were not prepared." He shrugged. "In retrospect, I'm not sure we could have been. You see, our society values individuality over everything else. We would rather be dead than live in an artificial prison of limited choice."

"But what about when the virus started killing people off? Wasn't anyone interested in collaborating for the common good?" I asked.

"There was talk of mandated quarantine, testing, social isolation, and the like, but it was all flatly rejected. I get that," he said, "people want the space to make their own decisions. But you might have thought there could be some element of balance and conformity to commonsense practices. Anyway, that did not occur here. There was a vaccine, but, again, no one could swallow a mandate. Plus, there were rumors of side effects, so vaccination was voluntary and, in the long run, not effective. You could not give that injection away here, nor convince people otherwise. They would rather die."

"Interesting. What happened next?" I asked.

"Well, almost everyone got the infection. Unfortunately, the toll was high. For the most part, everyone dismissed the alarm because, initially, the existence of a virus was labeled a hoax. It was business as usual, but then as the contagion spread and more people died, it became impossible to deny it any longer. But then many labeled this so-called virus an assault by those who wanted to destroy our ways of life. A civil war erupted. Easier to kill one another than admit we were wrong."

I shook my head. The virus seemed to really bring out

the character of the populations who had to deal with it in Fermion's wake.

"The combined toll of the pandemic and war was astounding," Louis continued. "If I had known that Fermion was responsible, I could have told them there would be no defense against a Janusian virus because it presents a different face constantly. Over time, people realized that the war was worse than the virus, so the fighting ended with the agreement that it was our right to disagree with one another and preserve self-determination. There is not much left," he said, waving his hand to the south, where the town had been. "The planet is a dangerous place — the virus, on the one hand, and the people trying to survive, on the other. Infrastructure collapsed, as you learned on the flight; we are all on our own. Mostly, I am left alone and live here with my dogs. I officiate at funerals or an occasional wedding. I pretty much know everyone back here. People bring food. We gather and have fellowship in the forest."

"I see," I replied.

The next thing I recall, I awoke inside my sleep sack. I was dressed as a flight attendant.

CHAPTER 14

Asleep at the Wheel of Fortune

The vice president was summoned to the White House for a meeting with the president's personal physician and the first lady to discuss a "problem."

President Workman was conspicuously absent. Vice President Cole invited the small, circumspect doctor and Melissa, the president's wife, into his office. The taciturn little man proceeded to explain that the first lady was complaining that the president was acting strangely, possibly suffering from the pressures of managing the country and coping with the worldwide pandemic.

Melissa nodded. "He has had severe insomnia, and when he does manage to sleep a few minutes, he is tormented by night terrors. He has been sleepwalking our apartment. It's just awful what he's going through."

Cole took it all in. This was sobering news. Just when the country needed their president to be strong and resolute, it seemed he was physically not up to the task.

The first lady then reported that John was "not the same." "He watches the news and his social media accounts constantly, rarely gets any quality sleep, and sometimes bolts awake, screaming, 'Leave me alone! You are already dead!' I have no idea who he is talking to!"

Cole felt a growing concern for his friend and colleague. He and President Workman had been friends long before they were politicians. Cole quickly sifted through his impressions of his latest interactions with the president. And in retrospect, yes, John was acting strangely. He seemed haunted but driven.

The physician went on to acknowledge that it was widely appreciated that no president led a particularly healthy lifestyle. It was a calculated risk willfully accepted by the commander in chief and those around him, but not necessarily by their spouses and families. The stress and the behavioral and dietary responses to it took their toll, as attested by the photographs that chronicled an accelerated aging process incurred by presidents moving through their tenure.

"Such an existence is challenging," the doctor said carefully, "with constant high-pressure meetings, many interruptions, poor sleep, and little time for exercise. Most meetings are catered and promote a seemingly sanctioned form of stress eating. Although the president's meals are expertly prepared, fine dining three or four times daily is a challenge for the waistline and cholesterol levels."

Cole nodded. He was well aware of the obstacles to good health a high-level governmental position posed, let alone John's role at the pinnacle.

"And John has a sweet tooth, you know," Melissa said. The physician's tone turned reproving. "He is overweight and prediabetic. And he is overdue for his medical exam." He turned to Cole and made the appeal: "If you can convince President Workman to show up for his examination, then perhaps I can talk to him about stress reduction?"

Cole nodded. "Thank you, doctor. Of course, I'll talk to John and advise him to look after his health, the first step of which is a consultation with you."

Of course, President Workman canceled the appointment, citing lack of time and that a more important urgent meeting had preempted it. But the next week, during an address to the Senate, it became obvious he was ill. He got lost in the conversation and was unable to speak, save for incomprehensible babbling punctuated by requests to be left alone. He kept repeating the phrase "go away."

Secret Service whisked him away to an adjoining conference room, and after about five minutes, his mind seemed to clear up. Seemingly intact, he returned to the chambers, faced the senators, and declared he was fine. "Nothing at all to be concerned about, my fellow Americans. My blood sugar was low. I just needed a doughnut," he said.

Later that afternoon, the presidential physician suggested that he slow things down, consider delegating some of his tasks to Vice President Cole and the White House staff, and submit to testing, which never happened. At that point, the infectious disease specialist and White House physician deemed it essential to sequester the president and vice president in separate quarters and for them to work remotely. The legislators moved quickly to provide financial relief for unemployed persons and struggling businesses. The economy went into a tailspin and headed into a recession.

Then the unthinkable happened. The vice president was contacted by the White House staff, who informed him that the president had fallen gravely ill and was being taken to the hospital. The president's aide arranged a private video conference.

President Workman's good-natured face appeared on-screen looking haggard, but his cheerful demeanor seemed undeterred. "Robert, apparently, I have this virus thing. The tests are positive. I am having a hard time catching my breath and have a high fever. Heads-up! If I get much worse, and especially should I require a ventilator, I will not be able to continue to work. I need you…to take command…for a while. I hereby delegate…you." He was barely able to finish his last sentence.

"Okay," said Robert. "Don't worry. I have your back.

You focus on getting well quickly, John."

"Thanks, good buddy." His voice was wheezy. "You know what to do. I will see you on the other side of this," said the president.

When the call disconnected, Cole immediately contacted his wife. "Honey, John is really sick, and I'm to assume the office of president until he gets well. I need you by my side." He explained that the Secret Service would be by to pick her up shortly. "Can you call Melissa, please? Tell her that she and the kids should remain in their quarters in the West Wing. Tell her John, and all of them, are in our prayers. But unfortunately, because we must remain sequestered, we can't be there with them. You and I will be staying in the East Wing and working remotely. Honey, can I ask you to pack up a few things and meet me here?"

Within the hour, the wire crackled with the news and the marquee in Times Square flashed the headlines. The world watched as Vice President Cole took the oath of office and assumed the presidency.

Later that night, he would confide to his wife his regrets that he and John had possibly underestimated the pandemic and that they should have taken it more seriously. They had been too focused on economics. The new president retired for the night but rested poorly, an unfortunate harbinger of his future.

The next morning's briefing started with a report of

President Workman's worsening condition. He was now on mechanical ventilation, with the world's experts on infectious disease and pulmonary medicine managing his treatment. Messages of condolences and support poured in from around the globe.

The new president summoned his staff in an effort to get a grasp on the enormity of the global situation. Meanwhile, the physicians lamented Workman's worsening oxygen levels. The X-rays of his lungs resembled a snowstorm. Before this illness knocked him down, he was a strong man. His body struggled mightily with high fevers, low blood pressures, and falling kidney function. Initially, the doctors predicted it would take him about three weeks to recover. Their goal was to support him through that time period, and he was given experimental treatments.

Wars of all types, whether fought by land, sea, air, or in the theater of the human body, produce collateral damage. An overzealous defense waged by the immune system can render an organ crippled like the scorched earth of the battlefield. Workman's doctors struggled with the balancing act. Soon he was turned on his stomach to improve the transport of oxygen in his damaged lungs. This maneuver worked for a few days, after which his oxygen levels were no longer sustainable. The experts had no other options except an artificial lung to circulate and oxygenate the blood outside the body. It's a very effective treatment for the short term and sometimes a lifesaving procedure that gives the lungs a rest, potentially allowing them to heal. Personally, Cole was in favor of doing everything possible for the ailing president, but he would leave the ultimate decision to former First Lady Melissa. At the same time, he turned his attention to the immediate and pressing tasks of balancing the people's physical health and the country's economic well-being, what he termed his great "pandilemma."

Acting President Cole, inundated with the tasks of managing the country amid the pandemic, coordinated a national response along multiple fronts. He assembled a pandemic task force that met twice daily for briefings and recommendations. The difficult decisions would be his while his friend and colleague, lying in the best intensive care unit in the world, remained a poignant reminder.

He was also quoted as saying, "When the house is on fire, it is difficult to think about the future." Like a professional athlete, you are only as good as your last game. Initially, control measures seemed like common sense: staying home when you're sick and avoiding others; washing your hands. Wearing masks was something surgeons did; sanitizing everything and wearing a mask, unless you were getting chemotherapy, was the behavior of germaphobes.

It was a bitter pill to swallow when the public health officials started shutting down society. Unemployment skyrocketed, and the economy tanked. Legislative relief packages, largely bipartisan, were required. Not everyone complied with the recommendations or felt it was within their civil rights to do so. With the arrival of the second, third, and fourth waves, people became weary, and the social dysfunction characteristic of epidemics throughout the ages manifested.

—

John Workman was weaned off the machines that had kept him alive; however, his body bore the devastating residual damage of the virus, precluding his return to office. This necessitated the ascension of the third person in the line of succession, the Speaker of the House of Representatives, who was sworn into the office as Acting Vice President. Robert Cole had an addition built onto the presidential home for his friend and the former president, whom he visited daily. The country looked to a vaccine for salvation and continued to struggle on all fronts.

It was not too long before the stress of the presidency would exact its toll. First, the dreams started. Cole's nights were plagued by visions of coffins, stacked and numbered so as to facilitate retrieval, methodically buried in large generic graveyards. Faceless masses were weeping over stricken loved ones. Streets were empty of the normal bustle of a thriving economy.

Only after the president started falling asleep during meetings — coffee no longer helping — did he call his physician. It was decided that he had sleep apnea, and it was preferable to start CPAP therapy rather than medications. Although it took a while to adapt to the technology, the first lady was thrilled that the snoring bear had been quieted. The president spoke of his love-hate relationship with the technology and admitted that at times he would toss his headgear across the room. He acknowledged, however, that he was more rested and functioning better during waking hours.

One afternoon, he went to see his disabled friend and former president in the annex. Cole's official stance was that "President Workman is welcome here, and we will care for him as long as I am in charge — with his wife Melissa's consent, of course." He sat beside his friend, who was resting in a recliner, his body surrounded and supported by fluffy pillows.

"Good morning, John. You look great," he said. There was no response from the normal-appearing yet comatose former president. "Well, things are a mess, John," Cole continued. "The pandemic marches forward largely unabated, unemployment is twenty-five percent, we have passed three relief bills, and there is a lot of red ink! We are hoping the vaccine will be our salvation, and, oh yeah, I have sleep apnea." Cole leaned closer to the still figure by his side. "I know you are in there, John." He patted John's arm. "I will visit again soon, hang in there, buddy."

CHAPTER 15

—

Lost in Space

M y second deployment was wrapping up. The prospects were bittersweet because it was unlikely that I would be assigned to a third tour of duty at the space station.

Like a rodent confined to cramped quarters, I had become accustomed to the modest accommodations of the space station. The trade-off, of course, was the magnificent view of the universe, larger than the biggest Montana sky.

I spent a lot of time in our observatory chamber, which was mostly constructed of space glass. We had a number of onboard telescopes that gave me an unlimited opportunity to observe the heavens, satisfying my interests in astrophotography. The pictures were spectacular. I could hardly wait to share them with my friend Carlos Gonzales.

On a video chat, I notified him of my imminent homecoming and hope for a visit. "How are things at the laboratory and observatory?" I queried.

He said they were operating on a skeleton crew but he continued his work studying the Large Magellanic Cloud — one of the magnificent wonders of the southern sky.

When I asked him about the "object," he said that when the vegetation and wildlife around the laboratory where it was housed started dying off in large numbers, they had evacuated the lab. It looked as if the area was suffering some sort of delayed effect of irradiation, so the area had been abandoned as off-limits. Drone surveillance showed other disturbing changes at the site. Carlos shared a few-second video clip over the link so I could see.

The object had been stored in a concrete bunker where it was placed in the center of a room approximately 100 square meters in size. Astonishingly, the video revealed that the floor had collapsed into a sinkhole, and it looked like the rest of the structure was soon to follow. The container was no longer visible; the hole now resembled a crater.

"I was really surprised," Carlos said. "I didn't think the laboratory would have been built on such unstable geography. As you know, telescopes are built on deeply secured piers secured to the bedrock."

I nodded in agreement. "Interestingly, I have learned something about the object," I replied. "I suggest you stay far away from that site. It is contaminated. I will explain it all to you when I see you. I am returning to Earth on the fourteenth and have two weeks of quarantine. Then I'll be down to see you."

"Okay, I look forward to your visit. *Estar a salvo, mi amigo,*" he replied.

I wished him well, too, and signed off.

About the time I thought I needed to speak with the Janus, I found myself bathing in the yellow warmth of North County, face-to-face with Louis McKay.

"I have been asked to relay this message," he said, and then his voice changed into the same moderated tone I had heard in my head when the Janus spoke to me on the star deck. "We have found Maia. In exchange for her father's life, she now exists in a state of quantum superposition. She agreed to this on that fateful day in New York City. She can be observed and thusly defined whenever medical devices called cardiac defibrillators are activated. Maia's dimension shifting proved to be the signal we detected and the start of the trail that led us to you in our investigation. More signals are emanating from a great number of beings who, while attempting to complete their journey, remain trapped in a cosmic purgatory."

I was ecstatic! "That's fantastic news," I said to Louis, though I assumed I was speaking to the Janus. "Although I do not fully comprehend the situation, Maia said in her last communication that she was okay. I knew we would find her someday!" I let out a whoop of joy. "I am forever grateful, in your debt. Thank you for that information. When can I see her?"

Louis's face remained impassive. "She is everywhere, appearing occasionally here, and sometimes there, and everywhere a defibrillator is in use."

"All right, then, although I am not entirely sure what that means. As we agreed, I have knowledge concerning the whereabouts of the horizon modulator and probably Fermion."

"We are grateful for your assistance," the collective voice chimed. "Although Maia cannot return to her previous life, you may choose to join her. The universe has suffered greatly. We propose restitution."

Louis sat quietly for a few minutes, after which he started speaking again, only in his voice. "They're gone."

"What was that all about?" I asked.

"Well, it appears that they are offering you and Maia a new existence together," he said encouragingly. "Probably with them, between the light and dark sides of the universe, where you can experience both. But you will not have a physical presence or body; you will no longer be visible to you or those looking for you on Earth. They are also proposing closure and healing for those lost in the pandemic. The beings trapped in the in-between status seem to be the source of the remaining dimension-shifting signals the Janus are detecting."

"Well, that's a pretty comprehensive package," I said. "As an astronaut, I have taken many risks that could have resulted in my death. The wager was, however, that it would not happen, and should it, well then, I'm gone, and usually instantaneously in this line of work. I never anticipated the day would come that someone would take me up on the wager or that I would have a choice."

"I totally understand," said Louis. "I chose a different path and will likely be in North County forever. I love it here, bathing in the yellow. I consider myself extremely blessed and fortunate. Your fate may lie elsewhere," said Louis. "You would 'die' in one realm to enter another, but then your wife is already there."

"Excellent point," I replied. "Tell them the answer is yes."

—

Space Command decided we would use the approaching orbital overlap nine days hence as the time for me and two other astronauts, one from Japan and one from the Netherlands, to return to Earth. Each of us in this newly formed three-person crew, veterans of the space station, had exhausted the maximum allowable time in space. We began intense preparation for our final exit.

On departure day, we entered the reusable landing vehicle (RLV) and commenced with the undocking and separation sequences. Everything went smoothly. As we distanced ourselves from the space station, it soon became indistinguishable from the stars shining in the darkness of space.

The pilot oriented the shuttle and fired the orbital maneuvering engines for the reentry burn. All sequences went smoothly, but then a velocity alert blazed across the screens. Calculations suggested that the RLV we were in was approaching the atmosphere with too much speed, which would cause us to skip off the exosphere and into deep space.

As flight engineer, I knew what must be done and told the other crew that I would troubleshoot the fuel control valves at the rear of the RLV.

I radioed my colleagues from the escape pod. "I found the problem. It appears that a valve was frozen closed." I paused, gathering my thoughts. Taking a monumental leap of faith, knowing the Janus were now in control and that I would soon be with Maia, I said, "It has been nice working with you, gentlemen. When I separate from the shuttle, the counterthrust will slow you down enough for reentry. Do not unduly lament my departure. It has been an honor to serve with all of you. Thank you. I will reside in the heavens — there is no greater place for an astronomer."

Leaving no time for debate, I charged the thruster and then blasted off, carrying the excess kinetic energy away with me as I watched the shuttle disappear into the upper level of the Earth's atmosphere.

—

On Earth, the world gasped and watched the fireworks of a spacecraft coming in faster than theoretically possible.

In the middle of the night, the communicator that sat on the nightstand next to Carlos Gonzales's bed blared an emergency alert, startling him awake. An urgent message flashed on the screen: "Carlos, this is William. Get out immediately. Look at these coordinates. A meteor is headed your way."

Carlos leaped from his bed and sprinted to his telescope. He pointed it to the coordinates William had shared and confirmed the incoming meteor. A bright spark suddenly appeared in an area of previously dark sky. Trusting fully in William's warning that the laboratory would be the impact site, he hastily gathered his keys, his canteen, and a jacket and raced to his truck. The engine roared to life amid the nighttime racket of the teeming forest, and Carlos peeled out, knowing that he needed to quickly distance himself from the region.

About an hour later, on the western horizon, the object became visible to the unaided eye and grew brighter with each passing minute. Suddenly, the light was quenched and replaced by a black funnel cloud. The column of darkness pierced the sky as it descended upon the observatory that Carlos had just abandoned. His ears shuddered at the sound of a deafening explosion that heralded the arrival of a shockwave that knocked him to the ground, where he remained praying.

—

Of course, I knew that my escape module would be seen by people on Earth as a meteor streaking across the southern sky. This would be the final reentry of my earthly existence. I led the Janus directly to the horizon modulator in Argentina.

Then, with their help, I warped through space-time and crossed the event horizon into the singularity through the gravity portal the Klabyau had opened for me. Simultaneously, Fermion within the horizon modulator attempted to escape by riding the resulting gravity wave.

I, therefore, found myself shoulder to virtual shoulder with a most unlikely travel companion, the thief of an entire galaxy. Thankfully, we encountered vastly different outcomes upon emergence on the other side.

Fermion fell into the trap set by the Janus and the Klabyau, and I continued upon a most celestial journey to a better fate.

CHAPTER 16

House Reordered

J ust after 2 a.m., President Cole's communicator lit up with an urgent, flashing alert. He had not been sleeping, so he sat up in bed and read the message. He and the presidential physician were being summoned to the White House annex. President Workman had fallen. He had tumbled from his wheelchair and was found lying unresponsive on the floor.

Cole hastily tied his robe around his middle and rushed to the West Wing in his slippers. When he padded into the room, he was confronted by an unfathomable sight. A man in an astronaut's suit materialized while a woman with blue-green hair kneeled next to the former president. And, a tall man with a salt-and-pepper braided beard stood behind them. Millions of COVID souls — he recognized them from his vivid, disturbing dreams — stood peacefully in a circle around the characters in the middle. All were enveloped in the warmth of golden yellow light.

"Oh God," William proclaimed as his presence stabilized. There was Maia, hovering over President Workman, having just delivered a 200-joule countershock with an AED. William ran toward Maia, and President Cole rushed toward John Workman. But then their approach slowed to a stop — they were frozen and unable to move as time stood still.

Louis McKay, his face impassive, stepped to the center of the circle. "We are the Janus," he said in an otherworldly voice. "Upon the authority and direction of the Source, the Creator of All, we have captured the perpetrator of this celestial plague and have restored the eleventh-dimensional galaxy to its rightful owners. In accordance with our agreements, Maia and William Preston shall exist everywhere in the universe in superposition. Presidents Robert Cole and John Workman, both good souls, shall read the names of the deceased, recognizing them for their ultimate sacrifice in the wake of this wrongful plague. The departed will have the opportunity to say goodbye to their families, freeing them from the bonds of their previous lives. It is decreed."

EPILOGUE

—

I n its desperate and chaotic state, the world would not
notice the supposed demise of one astronaut, or so I
thought. I was surprised to witness the outpouring of love
when the public — surely suffering more with their own
personal tragedies — mourned my loss from the world.
From our vantage point — which was no one point at all —
Maia and I could observe the goings-on of the universe, and
especially what was happening on our beloved home planet.

Space Command assured my family, as well as Heather
and Angelo, that there would be a full investigation into
the crash of the escape pod that led to my "death." The
engineers and scientists pored over the data for months.
Their research would reveal that the RLV carrying the
other two members of my crew successfully deployed its
parachutes and had landed in New Zealand.

Around the same time as the RLV's landing, apparently,
the planetary interferometers had gone off the scale
when they detected a massive gravitational event, which
was confirmed at several independent sites. The source,
however, could not be located. The Earth spewed a column

of material 500 kilometers into space — unknown to the planet's scientists, this matter flowed directly into and was completely consumed by the gravity portal the Klabyau had opened. The resulting massive Antarctic crater was so deep that molten magma arose from its depths and filled it from below as if healing a puncture wound in Earth's crust. The meteorite crater and presumed internment site of one U.S. astronaut William Preston, which bears my name, remains visible from outer space.

It would take many years for the world to recover, but gradually society, greatly altered, reopened. Presidents Cole and Workman could be found perpetually on the National Mall reading the names of those who had perished in the pandemic. Soon, they were joined by the heads of state from other countries and members of the clergy, with representation from every church and denomination.

With each passing day, as more and more COVID souls were freed, the former president's night terrors proportionally improved, as did his health. People returned to the restaurants and gymnasiums; once again, the theaters were full, and music blared from the arenas.

My good friends Heather and Angelo negotiated the latter years of lockdown gracefully, always contributing to the greater good, even if remotely from the lakeshore of Heather's ancestral home. Angelo would reopen his restaurant, which inarguably serves the finest food in this universe, and Heather's company would begin manufacturing the new defibrillators. She might not have consciously known that her best friend Maia "lives" within them, but she placed Maia's image on the case in honor of my father-in-law Frank's and the many other lives the devices would save.

Angelo's family's winery each year would produce a limited quantity of a ceremonial red blend he named "Asystole" — in honor of Maia and me! He always said we had heart. At Heather's suggestion, each bottle would prominently display Maia's likeness, and the proceeds would be donated to The Kind Spot Foundation established by Frank. Every year, Heather and Angelo would celebrate the season with a toast to us.

Finally, I am happy to say that their son Mark decrypted my hard drive and retrieved this file. What he does with the story remains to be seen. But I do believe that he will somehow help me fulfill my dream of becoming a published author, even if it is posthumously.

Maia and I reside with the Janus, keeping watch over the universe. Who would believe this Montana boy has visited every galaxy and nebula in the universe? I can assure you that I have done so. But across all those heavens, I have never found any as captivating as Maia's blue-green eyes and hair.

—

It was past midnight when Mark finished reading the last screen of William's story and closed the lid of the laptop. He sat there for a minute, rubbing his fingers across the decals of galaxies and nebulae. An idea was taking shape in his mind. Suddenly, he grabbed his communicator and started tapping away.

The next afternoon, Heather and Angelo strolled along the lake's edge hand in hand. What a bittersweet time, enjoying the solitude but also mourning the tragic cause of its existence. Heather's communicator vibrated in her pocket. She tapped the speaker button.

An automated message droned into the humid air: "This is a recorded message from the Galactic Press: In order to submit a manuscript for publication, an adult over the age of eighteen must open an account on your behalf. Please visit our website for details regarding our available services. Thank you for your request. We look forward to working with you. We appreciate your interest in the Galactic Press." And then the line disconnected.

Heather and Angelo looked at each other, puzzled. "I think we better go talk to Mark," he said.

They headed up to the house and found Mark hunched over William's laptop.

"Anything you want to tell us?" Angelo asked.

Mark gave them a sheepish grin. "Well, yes, a lot! William didn't die, and neither did Maia!"

They looked at him, stunned.

He continued without skipping a beat: "You should reopen your restaurant, Dad, and, Mom, what would you say about putting a picture of Maia on your AEDs? Those are great ideas, right? And let me tell you, we're gonna survive this pandemic, and things will — "

"Whoa! Hold on, bud, what's all this? How do you know?" Heather stepped closer and put her hand to Mark's forehead, feeling for heat.

He brushed her fingers away and shoved the laptop at her. "Here! You guys have got to read this! It's William's complete story, and I think we should make it into a book!"

It didn't take them long to read the entire tale, and then they sat together on the couch, contemplating the implications.

"Well?" said Mark excitedly.

"Well," Angelo said slowly.

"We can publish under a pen name to protect William's privacy, right?" Mark suggested. "What do you say? Can I? Can I, please?"

Angelo looked at Heather, and she nodded. "Okay, son, let's go for it!"

Mark leaped into the air, pumping his fist to the ceiling. "Yeah! Thanks, Dad! Thanks, Mom!" He leaned in and gave them both a peck on the cheek. Then he straightened, sat down in front of the laptop, and cracked his knuckles. "Hmm, I think this author needs a name. How about Mark Goode."

—

Millions of years later, space travelers originating from the Sombrero Galaxy approached the outer bounds of the Milky Way. Their research had suggested the possibility that life might exist in a neighboring galaxy.

As their spacecraft de-cloaked, it slowly advanced toward one of many orbs that delineated the edges of this alien galaxy. Posted every ten parsecs, the orbs transmitted the following message: *"Warning!! COVID Galaxy ahead. Do not enter. Warning!! COVID Galaxy ahead. Do not enter."*

The viral pandemic that swept the Milky Way had resulted in the sociological superposition of life and death. For the most part, this inconvenient truth was difficult for humanoids to accept because they preferred to be in one state or the other.

Humanity, therefore, had to reconcile its innate need to socialize, explore, and be free with the scientific realities of medicine, infectious disease, and the epidemiology of the pandemic or potentially face extinction. The survival of humankind hung in the balance. The search for interstellar life would have to await the outcome. Meanwhile, the orbs encircling the galaxy would remain in place, a warning to any others who might risk visiting the afflicted galaxy.

Over the eons, with no contact with any life-form from outside the galactic bounds, it did indeed seem like we were alone in the universe.

But are we?

Made in the USA
Monee, IL
24 September 2021